Unfair Exchange

Also by Marian Babson

Unfair Exchange.

Marian Babson

Walker and Company
New York

First published in the United States of America
in 1986 by the Walker Publishing Company, Inc.

Library of Congress Cataloging-in-Publication Data

Babson, Marian.
Unfair exchange.

I. Title.
PS3552.A25U5   1986   813'.54   86-11052
ISBN 0-8027-5660-3

Printed in the United States of America

10 9 8 7 6 5 4 3 2 1

CHAPTER 1

THE ECHO of Caroline's laughter rang in her ears long after Zita had replaced the receiver. Caroline's laugh was a carillon of silver bells, a graceful cascade of amusement that rose and fell with perfect control and enchanted any listener – particularly male – who wasn't completely tone deaf. But, to Zita, Caroline's laughter was always faintly mocking. Just as Caroline's portrait over her fireplace was a constant reminder that Caroline had been first in David's life – and in David's heart.

Zita stood up abruptly and moved about the room in what David called one of her 'fell swoops'. She pushed a chair a few inches back, changed a vase of roses from the table to the windowsill, tidied a pile of magazines, then took a deep breath, some of the tension gone. Perhaps it was silly, but the quiet little motions asserting her chatelaineship reassured her. As did just standing there and surveying the pleasant room.

The solid welcoming sprawl of the Victorian sofa, the glint of the copper oil lamp (now converted to electricity), the warm dark mahogany glow of the card table, all soothed her.

Disconcertingly, she suddenly wondered if this passion of hers for Victoriana had anything to do with Caroline. Was it symptomatic of a longing for past halcyon days, when a second wife could be sure that her predecessor had had the decorum to waste away from consumption or be thrown from a horse? Life must have been so much simpler when a man's first wife lay safely in a peaceful grave underneath a weeping willow tree, deeply mourned, but decently departed; rather than rushing around flauntingly, belligerently alive – and insisting on being a friend of the family.

Worse, Caroline was eternally turning up in the gossip columns (her current escort was some slightly shady Greek who owned a chain of gambling clubs) and being photographed at First Nights and Society Charity Balls. During the Season, it was a rare week when one wasn't reminded of Caroline at least twice. Zita had quite mastered the art of passing it off with a casual remark when any friends mentioned it, but she wondered sometimes if David minded. She had never quite dared to ask.

Once again the portrait over the fireplace drew her eyes. It was Caroline at her best, soft and fragile, with fluffy blonde hair, and the face of a dreaming girl. It was impossible to think that David might not still care, might not still have occasional twinges of regret that he had let her slide away. No matter how badly she had behaved. Men could forgive a lot when a woman was as flawlessly beautiful as that. And David was an artist. Beauty mattered more to him than it might to other men.

David. She wished he were here now. An anticipatory pang of loneliness caught at her throat. He wasn't far – at the moment. Only at the American

Embassy seeing about his visa. But, by this time tomorrow, he would be on his way three thousand miles
away – to remain for three long weeks.

The opportunity was too good to miss, of course.
He would be doing the preliminary sketches for six
murals commissioned by one of the big industrial com-
bines which made a practice of encouraging rising
young artists in order to project a public relations
image of involvement with the Arts. He would have
no time, really, for her – even if the budget had been
able to stretch to include a ticket for her. In his inde-
pendent way, David had refused to accept an airline
ticket from the corporation concerned, feeling that it
was better not to be under obligation to them, in case
they rejected his sketches. In the way that such inde-
pendence can interreact on an American firm, they
had immediately written and raised the original offer
for his work.

But three weeks was a long time to be alone. The
house, a tiny pseudo-Georgian cottage arching its bow
window into a quiet Islington square, was not quite
large enough to provide her with a full day's work
every day. Especially now that it was so close to
completely furnished. Nor would haunting the antique
markets for the bits and pieces that would provide the
finishing touches.

Perhaps it was time to think about taking a job
again. At least, a part-time one which would keep her
occupied while David was away. But David was bitterly
sensitive to any implication that he might not be able
to support a wife in adequate style. Which was another

legacy from the days when he was married to Caroline.

So many roads led inexorably back to Caroline. So many indelible stains and scars which might take years to fade – if they ever did. It might help if Caroline were not somehow so innocently ingenuous that it was impossible to hate her completely.

Zita shook her head; she was falling into the mood when she wished to sit down and spend a few hours mentally analysing Caroline. It was a pointless exercise at best, and she had no time for it now – she had carelessly allowed herself to be manoeuvred into meeting Caroline for lunch. She hadn't really wanted to, but Caroline had been so insistent. And, somehow, Caroline always managed to get her own way.

The Savoy Grill wasn't too crowded but, for a moment, Zita didn't see Caroline. Then Caroline raised a hand in greeting and Zita realized that, unconsciously, she had been looking for that great drifting cloud of silver-gilt hair. But Caroline had tucked it all up into a pale grey turban, which matched her pale grey linen suit, just as the pink scarf at her throat matched the large pink sunglasses through which she viewed the world at the moment.

She frowned slightly as Zita sat down, and Zita promptly felt overdressed, overdone, and far too vivid in the red silk dress which had seemed to set off her short curly black hair and pale complexion so well at Islington parties. 'You look like a flame,' David had said when she first wore it. But David was not here, and Caroline looked like the pale subtle smoke of spring bonfires. Zita slumped into her chair and tried to fight the conviction that smoke was infinitely more appealing than a blatant blaze.

'I've ordered,' Caroline said. 'I know you like steak – underdone, of course.'

Perhaps she would have ordered the steak anyway, but she would have liked a chance to look at the menu. 'That's very thoughtful of you,' Zita said carefully.

Caroline seemed to find her tone all right. 'Have a cigarette.' She tossed a packet of American cigarettes to Zita.

'Thank you.' Zita didn't quite catch the packet and retrieved it quickly from the floor, studying the printed health warning emblazoned along the side to cover her clumsiness. Smiling ruefully, Zita took out one of the cigarettes and lit it from the packet of matches at the table, before Caroline could flourish that gold lighter in her face.

'It's lovely to see you again.' The annoying thing was that Caroline actually seemed to mean it. No matter how long she had maintained a withdrawn silence, Caroline always gave the impression that it was other people who had been unavailable to her.

'You're looking very well.' It was as much as Zita could trust herself to say.

'I'm all right.' Caroline shrugged, and broke off to spend a few moments enchanting the wine waiter in French which was probably flawless. She didn't bother to consult Zita about the choice, and Zita knew that the order would be for something very chic, very expensive, and probably far too dry for her taste.

'I *never* see very much of you,' Caroline said accusingly. 'What do you *do* with yourself all day?'

'I keep busy,' Zita said. *And keep smiling*, she reminded herself, but it was difficult. Caroline always made it seem so plausible, natural – and inevitable – that they should meet, quite overlooking the awkwardnesses when they did. What, after all, did they have in common – except a husband?

'You've been quite busy yourself, I see by the papers.' Zita stubbed out the too-strong cigarette and scrabbled in her handbag for one of her own. 'A big new romance, isn't it?'

'Ummm,' Caroline unexpectedly grew thoughtful. 'We haven't had *that* much publicity, have we?'

'Oh no,' Zita offered the answer that seemed to be desired. 'No, I suppose I just noticed it more because – ' No, that was terribly gauche – but Caroline always turned her into an awkward schoolgirl – she abandoned that line of thought abruptly. 'He's terribly handsome.'

'He is, isn't he?' But Caroline's face grew darker. It must be time to change the subject but, having desperately grasped at this one, Zita found it impossible to think of another. It wasn't as though she and Caroline had so much to talk about – and she did not want to discuss David. Not right now. Not with Caroline – ever.

'What's his real name? All the newspapers ever call him is Xavier.'

'Oh, something Greek and unpronounceable.' Caroline shrugged it away. 'He always says Xavier is enough

of a name. I think he likes it, really. It means everyone
knows who he is. No one ever asks – Xavier *who?*'

The waiter loomed up beside them and began serving.
Zita had the impression that Caroline was glad to have
the conversation ended. Perhaps the current romance
wasn't going so well. It was becoming more noticeable
as the years wore on that although Caroline was very
good at *getting* men, she was a bit careless about
holding on to them. Already, since David, there had
been another brief marriage, a much-publicized fling
with a Brazilian millionaire, and now Xavier.

'Actually,' Caroline said, as the waiter moved away,
'that's rather a problem I have at the moment. Xavier,
I mean. I – I wanted your advice.'

She wanted more than advice. Zita abruptly lost all
taste for the delicious steak as she realized the purpose
of the luxury luncheon. Caroline wanted something
from her – or from David. Of course, now that she
thought back, they rarely did hear from Caroline when
life was going well for her. It was only when she was
at a loss for more exciting companions or when things
were going wrong, that she fell back on them – as
though they were her family.

'Yes?' Zita said cautiously.

'Well . . .' Caroline seemed to hesitate, then decide
to blurt out the truth. 'It's Fanny – I don't know what
to do about her . . . You know about Fanny?' She
slanted an uneasy glance at Zita. 'David *adored* her.'

'I'm sure he did.' Some response was called for. Zita
knew vaguely that Fanny was the child of Caroline's
first marriage to a major in the American Army. David

had not said anything much about Fanny, but then he never discussed his marriage to Caroline if he could avoid it. And probably he had not seen much of Fanny. The divorce had taken place in the United States (after Caroline had enjoyed an indiscreetly public interlude with an Austrian skiing instructor in Aspen, Colorado) and the Court had granted custody to the father. Not so much because of Caroline's escapade, but because the Court learned that the mother intended to return to England and felt that no American child should be uprooted from its heritage and tossed into the depravity of a European life. David had not met Caroline until her return and, therefore, could have had little to do with Fanny. But David *did* love children and, perhaps, if this commission went well . . .

'It couldn't have come at a worse possible time,' Caroline rushed on. 'Her father has been sent on some mission to India, and he thinks she ought to spend her summer holidays with me. So that we can have a chance to get better acquainted, he says. But also so that he and his wife can settle in comfortably before the family joins them. They're sending their own children to a summer camp.'

'It will be nice for you to see her again, won't it?' Zita was treading carefully, feeling that she was on the edge of some morass, which was about to gurgle and gulp at her feet and swallow her up.

'Oh, of course,' Caroline said quickly. 'That is, it *would* have been – but not right now. Right now, it puts me in the most awful position! You see, Xavier has invited me to join a small party on his yacht. We'll be cruising in the Med for a fortnight. Naturally, I *long* for Xavier to get to know Fanny – but a yacht isn't really the place.' She leaned across the table, widening her eyes pleadingly, and Zita felt the ground shift under her feet.

'A yacht sounds like a very good place to get acquainted with someone,' Zita said hastily. 'Quiet – and away from other distractions – ' She broke off, wondering abruptly just *how* small the party was intended to be.

'But children get restless – even the best of them,' Caroline said. 'And there's always the danger of their falling overboard. And – and – it's all happened so suddenly, I haven't had an opportunity to discuss it with Xavier and see how he feels about it, and – '

'Can't you cancel the cruise? Stay at home with Fanny?'

'Cancel – ?' Caroline looked suddenly like a child herself, one whose toys have just been snatched away. Her lower lip trembled. Whatever else she had thought of, she had never thought of losing her own treat. 'Oh, I couldn't. I couldn't possibly. It's out of the question. This party is terribly important.'

'I see,' Zita said slowly. Caroline and Xavier had been 'an item' for quite a long time now. Perhaps he was on the point of proposing – or perhaps the party was going to be a honeymoon. In which case, one certainly wouldn't want the child of an earlier marriage underfoot. At least – the groom probably wouldn't. And Caroline had never seemed very heavily burdened with maternal instincts. Oddly, Zita felt a little pang of sympathy for Fanny, so small, and so definitely not wanted on the voyage.

'It wouldn't be for long.' As though sensing weakness, Caroline pressed home her advantage. 'Only for three weeks, and then I'd take her for the rest of the summer. Oh, Zita, if you possibly could – I'd be forever grateful. Besides – ' in her eagerness, she went one step too far – 'you might be glad of the company while David is away.'

Now, who had told her that David was going to be away for three weeks? Zita raised an eyebrow, and Caroline was not slow to see that she had blundered.

'Well, he is, isn't he? I met him in Bond Street the other day. He mentioned it in passing. So, naturally, I thought you – You *are* her aunt – practically. Oh, dear – ' her eyes filled with tears – 'I've upset you. And I didn't mean to. I just thought it would be so nice for you both. And it would help me *so* much.'

A scene at the Savoy was the last thing Zita felt she could cope with right now. She simply wanted to go home and sit down quietly and try to decide just what this meant to her marriage. She wasn't jealous – not really. But David had not mentioned meeting Caroline the other day.'

'I'm not upset,' Zita said. 'It's all right.'

'Then you will!' Caroline glowed. 'You won't mind. Oh, I know you'll love her – '

'No, I didn't mean that,' Zita said hastily. 'I simply meant I'm not upset.'

'You are! You are!' Caroline wailed. 'And it's all my fault. I've done this so badly. I've been so clumsy – '

Her face brightened. 'If it's a question of money – ' She dived into her handbag, scrabbling through it frantically, and surfaced flaunting her chequebook.

It was the last straw. 'Money has nothing to do with it!' In fact, money had everything to do with it – David would never forgive her if she accepted a penny from Caroline. Perhaps Caroline realized that, and was baiting the trap more skilfully than she seemed. 'It's not a question of expense – '

'Oh, good. Then that's all right.' Caroline turned to the waiter, who had advanced with the bill when he saw her reach for her handbag. 'You don't mind? We can have coffee at the airport, if you like.'

'The airport?' Zita said faintly, realizing that Caroline must have arranged something with the waiter before she arrived. Otherwise, the bill would never have been presented in such a rush – and before coffee.

'Of course,' Caroline said. 'Oh – didn't I mention it? Fanny is there. We really ought to be getting along. We've kept her waiting quite long enough.'

CHAPTER II

CAROLINE DROVE as she behaved: outrageously, ignoring all rules, and caring nothing for public opinion. The car, obedient to her sudden whims, whiplashed around corners, slowed on empty streets, accelerated through heavy traffic, leapfrogged red lights. They left in their slipstream a wake of pale pedestrians and cursing motorists, to which Caroline seemed serenely oblivious.

After one vain attempt, Zita gave up trying to re-open the argument. She had been completely out-manoeuvred and was going to have a small house-guest for the next three weeks. That was all there was to that, and she had better try to look on the bright side.

For one thing, sight unseen, she sympathized with the child. Poor little thing, coming all this distance for a reunion with her mother and being casually shunted off into the care of a – to her – complete stranger. Zita determined to be a friend to Little Fanny. (Already she visualized a frail ethereal child with Caroline's candyfloss hair and enormous appealing eyes, frightfully shy and insecure – as children of divorce, tossed backwards and forwards between two sets of parents, so often were.) She acknowledged, too, the ignoble thought at the back of her mind that this might prove to David that she would make a better mother than Caroline.

Plunging down into the tunnel just outside Heathrow, the car seemed to hesitate momentarily as Caroline flicked a sideways glance at Zita. 'I *do* appreciate this, you know,' she said. 'I really do.'

And so you jolly well might, Zita thought. But the car leaped for the daylight at the end of the tunnel and, somehow, the moment when she might have spoken was lost.

Caroline veered expertly into the parking lot, braking much too hastily, and was out of the car before Zita could undo her safety belt. 'Come on,' she said impatiently. 'We don't want to keep Fanny waiting any longer.' She started away, flinging back over her shoulder, 'Number One Terminal.'

Zita had to run to catch up with her, wondering why she bothered. *She* was doing Caroline a favour, after all, but Caroline always managed to make it seem the other way around. She had no breath to protest with, however, and followed Caroline meekly into the terminal and up the stairs. Caroline might, she thought bitterly, at least look back over her shoulder again to make sure Zita hadn't been lost in the airport crowds, instead of forging ahead with the calm assurance that everything was going just as she had planned it.

Caroline pulled up so abruptly that Zita nearly walked into her. They had arrived. There was a cluster of comic books, small suitcases and airline bags heaped on both sides of a small form, but Caroline blocked her view of the child.

'There now,' Caroline said, with a brisk, wary con-

ciliatoriness, 'that didn't take so very long, did it?'
She stepped aside. 'Say hello to Auntie Zita – you're
going to visit her for a while.'

Two blazing hostile eyes raked Zita and dismissed
her with contempt. They switched to Caroline, with
scarcely less contempt, then the child went back to
the comic book she had been reading when they
approached.

'Fanny!' For once, Caroline seemed to have lost
command of the situation. 'Say hello to Auntie Zita!'

'Hello,' the child mumbled, not bothering to raise
her eyes again. As though to punctuate her indiffer-
ence, she turned the page of the comic.

'You're going to go home with Auntie Zita now.'
Caroline was wheedling, instinctively falling into the
technique which usually brought her success – at least
with the opposite sex. 'You'll like visiting her. She's
the lady who's married to Daddy David now. You
remember Daddy David, don't you?'

Fanny shrugged, monumentally unimpressed both
by the information and the syrupy voice in which it
was offered.

Zita found herself flinching at the enormity of the
task she had taken on. How could she – 'entertain'
was such an inappropriate word – how could she have
this ghastly child under her roof for the next three
weeks? And what – she felt a certain disenchantment
with Caroline's earlier assertions – what would David
say?

'If you'll excuse me a minute,' she said to Caroline.
'I think I ought to phone David and –'

'You haven't time,' Caroline said sharply. 'I mean,' she amended, as Zita stared at her, 'it's going to take you quite a while to get back to London. You'll have to start right away, if you don't want to get caught in the rush hour. The Tube is bad enough at the best of times.'

'The Tube?' Zita said unbelievingly.

'Oh, I'm terribly sorry – didn't I tell you? I won't be able to drive you back. You see, the party is starting today. We're all meeting at a pub in Marlow, then we'll board the yacht there, and sail out directly – so much more convenient than trying to bring it in to moorings anywhere along the London end of the river.'

Avoiding Zita's eye, Caroline stooped and expertly stripped the luggage labels off the cases on the floor. When she straightened, she had a small case and one of the airline flight bags in her hand. The sealed neck of a gin bottle peeped out of the top of the flight bag. 'Thank you for bringing these in for me,' she said, rather formally, to her daughter, who continued to ignore her.

'Just follow that ramp over there.' Caroline turned to Zita. 'It will lead you to the bus stop and the bus goes to the Tube station. There are signs. You can't miss your way.'

Her way had been lost since she answered the telephone that morning, but Zita was too taken aback by Caroline's temerity to argue the point.

'And don't worry about Fanny,' Caroline said. 'She has her own money. She won't be any trouble – I've spoken to her already and she understands. Make sure she pays her own way. Goodbye, darling.' She aimed a kiss at her daughter's bent head. 'I'll see you in three weeks. Goodbye, Zita.' Her lips grazed Zita's cheek. 'So good of you.' She smiled, waved, and incredibly, she was gone.

Now the child lowered her comic book and stared in the direction Caroline had vanished. Zita, too, looked after Caroline, feeling rather as though she had just been caught up in a hurricane. The trouble was that she was left with the debris to clear up. Warily, she turned towards Fanny and found the child looking directly at her.

'You've got egg on your face,' Fanny said.

Automatically, Zita raised her hand to her face before remembering that it was just an American expression. 'I suppose I have,' she said uncertainly.

'Everybody has,' Fanny said, 'when Caroline gets through with them.'

Was she speaking of herself, too? Zita felt a momentary sympathy. While not quite what she had expected, Fanny *was* a child and must feel doubly deserted, with her father going to India and shunting her off on to her mother, and her mother promptly shunting her off on to yet a third – unknown – person. No wonder the child seethed with hostility.

'Come along, then,' Zita said. 'I suppose we might as well start for home.'

'I'm not ready yet.' Fanny gave her a long, implacable look and returned to her comic book. 'I'm reading.'

Zita's sympathy abruptly disappeared. 'Stay here a moment, then. I'll go and make inquiries about catching one of the airport buses back to town.'

The child raised her head, alert as a forest animal sensing danger. 'Caroline said for us to take the Tube.'

'Caroline isn't here now.' And Caroline had had her gall, to desert them here, miles from town, calmly suggesting the most inconvenient journey back.

'Okay. okay.' Elaborately, the child folded her comic book, added it to the pile at her feet, and picked the pile up, stuffing them into her bulging flight bag. 'I'm coming. Follow the ramp, Caroline said, and we'll get to the bus.'

Since the threat of disobeying Caroline had moved Fanny, when she had seemed prepared to balk at moving at all, Zita abandoned argument about the airport bus. Probably Fanny, although she wouldn't admit it, was thrilled by the idea of the Tube. There was no underground railway, Zita remembered reading, anywhere in California. It would undoubtedly put her one-up on all her friends.

Zita stooped and picked up the two cases. Fanny immediately wrestled to get possession of them. '*I* can carry them,' she said. 'You don't have to bother.'

She couldn't, and carry the flight bag as well. Zita let her stagger a few steps with the entire load, then reached for the larger case. 'I'll take one, and you can manage the others.' She tugged firmly at it, and Fanny had to release it.

'Wait a minute,' Fanny said, as they came opposite the plastic space capsules, revolving enticingly to display choice selections of British luxury goods for export. 'I want to get something.'

'I'm not sure – ' Zita began.

'You don't have to worry,' Fanny flashed defensively. 'I've got my own money. *I* can buy it.'

'I was going to say, I'm not sure that we can carry anything more.'

'*I* can carry it!' Fanny set her cases down and rummaged importantly in her handbag. 'Here, hold these a minute!' She removed a jumbled top layer of wadded Kleenexes and sticks of gum and shoved them into Zita's hand, then started excavating through a second layer of lipsticks (several shades) and small bottles of duty-free French perfumes.

Now that it was thus drawn to her attention, Zita realized that the musky odour she had thought part of the general airport atmosphere was emanating from the small body before her. Not only that, but the peculiarly pink blur of Fanny's mouth gave evidence of lipstick applied and then scrubbed off, either by an irate parent, or because the child herself had suddenly thought better of it. But Caroline had not had time to do any scrubbing – nor, probably, the inclination, had she even noticed.

'*Here* it is,' Fanny said with satisfaction. She pulled out a bulging change purse. Beneath it, Zita could glimpse at the bottom of the handbag, a large wodge of assorted currency, dollars and pounds jammed gloriously together as a sort of foundation layer for the chaos above.

'Okay!' She snatched her other loot out of Zita's

hands, shovelling it back into her handbag, and snapped the bag shut. 'I'll be right back.'

Zita watched helplessly while the child marched over to the counter. At some point, she must put her foot down – but at what point and over what issue? Gloomily, she felt that Fanny had not yet begun to show her darker side. Does a spoilt child ever realize what a brat it is? Probably, by her own lights, Fanny was behaving as an ideal guest. Caroline had told her to pay her own way – and that was what she was doing.

Fanny had disappeared in the crowd. One moment she had been forging towards the cash register, the next moment she was nowhere to be seen. Fighting down panic, it occurred to Zita that there was more to being a parent than there seemed to be. Of course, one's own child would be much better brought up, and never, never –

But, where *was* Fanny? Could she have deliberately slipped away in order to follow Caroline back to the parking lot in the hope of being allowed to stay with her? Yet Fanny had seemed to receive the information that she was going to spend the next three weeks with Auntie Zita fairly stolidly. Fanny, in fact, seemed to have no great emotion about anything – except, possibly, getting her own way.

Then, shoving her way through the milling throng, Fanny surfaced and came towards her, carrying a large, incredible giraffe composed of what appeared to be spotted suede and with enormous false eyelashes coyly lowered to half-mast over iridescent green-gold eyes. Fanny was cradling it tenderly in her arms and Zita realized that she was really a child, after all. Perhaps the next few weeks might not be so bad.

'Okay.' Coming up to her, the blank indifferent mask slid over Fanny's face again. 'We can go now.' She bent, casually stuffing the toy into the top of the flight bag, and one had to be alert to see that she wasn't being so careless as she seemed.

'It's very pretty,' Zita said. 'What are you going to name it?'

'I don't know.' Fanny's face was completely shuttered now. Perhaps she had sounded too patronizing. It might be better to ignore the toy.

'I think we'd best find a telephone before we start back to London,' Zita said. 'I ought to call my husband –' She could not bring herself to say 'Daddy David'. She wondered if Fanny actually called him that, or whether it was Caroline's idea of a suitable name. 'He isn't expecting me to return with – a guest.'

Fanny flashed a bright, unexpectedly disconcerting look, but said nothing. Zita was left with the impression that Fanny realized more of the situation than seemed possible. Also, that there were several pertinent comments Fanny could contribute – if she chose. But she remained silent. Thankfully, Zita spotted a telephone booth nearby, and headed for it.

There was a long silence as Zita explained – or tried to. Then David said dangerously, 'Are you trying to tell me that you have allowed yourself to be landed with Fanny the Fiend?'

'But Caroline said you were terribly fond of . . .' Zita floundered, aware suddenly of how specious anything Caroline might say really was. 'I mean, don't you love – like . . . ?'

'Come home,' David said grimly. 'Obviously, it's too late for argument. Perhaps she's improved.'

Outside the phone booth, Fanny flattened her face against the glass and unfurled her tongue, waggling it derisively at Zita.

CHAPTER III

STRUGGLING UPHILL from the Angel, Fanny asked, 'Why haven't you got a car?'

It was approximately the fourteenth time the question had arisen in one form or another. Feeling rather frayed, Zita snapped, 'Because I can't drive.'

'But if you had a car, you'd learn to drive, wouldn't you?'

'Perhaps.'

'I'm going to get a car when I'm sixteen. My father promised me. I can drive some already. If you had a car, I could drive it for you now.'

'Over my dead body,' Zita muttered, wondering as much at the doting permissiveness of Fanny's father as at Fanny's calm assurance that she would actually reach the advanced age of sixteen, the way she behaved.

'Do you mean you wouldn't let me? You'd *have* to let me if you couldn't drive yourself. My father lets me drive *his* car in and out of the driveway. His *little* car, of course.'

'We turn here and cross the next street,' Zita said, doggedly refusing to be drawn into an argument over a hypothetical automobile.

'It's a long way, isn't it?' Fanny shifted her grip on her cases, panting slightly.

'You're just not used to walking.' Zita hardened her

heart. Fanny's genuinely childlike moments came too
infrequently to be effective. 'It's all that driving about
in the family limousine – I mean, the *little* car.' She
was immediately ashamed of herself. The trouble was
that Fanny reduced one to her own level.

'In any case,' she said, as they turned the final
corner, 'here we are. That's the house – the little one
with the bow window on the other side of the square.'
Her tone was apologetic, although the words were not,
but Fanny seemed to sense her meaning.

'It's a very pretty house,' Fanny said. 'I guess, maybe, you wouldn't have room for a car there, though.
I mean, there's no garage.' In her own way, Fanny was
tendering an apology also.

'Space is at a premium in London,' Zita said. 'One
is frightfully lucky to have a house, never mind a
garage.' The truce thus signed, they crossed the square
in amiable silence. For the first time, Zita began to feel
that Fanny might not be too much of a problem. The
feeling lasted until they entered the house.

David was waiting in the tiny entrance hall, thumb-
ing through an already-opened pile of afternoon post
on the console-table, trying to look as though he had
not been waiting for them to arrive.

'Oh, there you are,' he greeted inconsequentially.

'Sorry, darling.' Zita pecked at his cheek. 'It took
longer than I thought to get back here from the airport.'

Fanny dumped her cases at her feet and looked
around the hallway without comment or enthusiasm.
David looked at her, with equal lack of enthusiasm.

'Say hello to David,' Zita commanded, as the mutual silence lengthened. 'You do remember – ' it was no use, she would have to say it, it might be the only name Fanny knew him by – ' "Daddy David", don't you?' There, she had forced it out, but she felt slightly sick.

David glanced at her incredulously. He looked as though he might be on the point of retching himself.

Fanny turned fully and raked him with her long contemptuous gaze. 'Hello, stupid,' she said finally.

'Fanny!' Zita gasped in horror.

Fanny transferred the contemptuous gaze to her. 'Of course, he's stupid,' she said. 'All Caroline's husbands are stupid.'

'She has a point,' David admitted grimly.

'My father is, too.' Fanny said, with calm satisfaction.

'No doubt,' David said.

'Perhaps I'd best show you to your room,' Zita intervened hastily. If Fanny could so immediately reduce David, too, to her own level, Zita would rather not know about it. A bride of less than a year, she reminded herself hysterically, is still entitled to *some* delusions.

'Okay.' Fanny picked up her cases again, resisting David's efforts to take them. '*I* can carry them,' she said.

The room was light, bright and cheerful, at the front of the house overlooking the square. It had a bed, oak dresser and armchair. They would get around to furnishing it more completely later, but other rooms in the house took higher priority. The only guest to occupy the room so far had been Zita's sister on a rare visit from Devon during school holidays – and she had had no complaints.

'*This* isn't very much,' Fanny said. 'Don't you have any more furniture than this?' She flung open the closet door. 'There aren't even any coathangers.'

'I'll get you some,' Zita said, and retreated. Behind her, she heard Fanny sigh gustily and begin opening her cases.

David had come upstairs and was waiting in the hallway. They exchanged glances, then he followed her into their room and shut the door.

'You haven't really gone mad, have you?' he asked.

'I thought you'd be pleased.' Zita began collecting the coathangers strewn around the room from David's already-packed suits. 'Caroline said you were very fond of Fanny.'

'And you believed her?'

'Well, I hadn't seen Fanny then,' she said defensively.

'I should think not. That's really a child only a mother could love – and if she does, why hasn't *she* got her?'

'Caroline said she'll take her in three weeks, but she had to go on a yachting party – it seemed terribly important to her. If I hadn't taken the child, she might have just left her . . . anywhere. And I felt sorry for Fanny. It can't be easy to come to your mother for your summer holidays and find she doesn't even care, that she's going off somewhere else and leaving you.'

David crossed to stand before her. He put a finger under her chin and tilted her face to kiss her gently. 'You *are* a mug, aren't you?' he said.

'I suppose so,' she admitted, 'but – '

'Hey!' Fanny's voice shouted. 'Are you going to be all night getting those hangers? I *need* them.'

'Coming,' Zita called. 'Really,' she assured David, 'I'm sure she'll improve. She's just unsettled at the moment. She was almost human coming up the hill.'

'All right, all right,' David laughed. 'At any rate – ' he sobered – 'I'm just as glad you won't be alone here while I'm away. If I know Fanny, she'll keep you too busy to be lonely.'

'I'll still miss you,' Zita said.

But David's attention had wandered. He looked roofwards, where a glass-sided studio had been built across half the width of the house at the back. Inside, the easel, the pallettes, the twisted tubes of paint, the canvasses stacked against one wall, all would be hostage to an inventive child with little regard for another's property. A door opened directly on to the roof itself, presenting a further temptation – and hazard – for an exploring little mind.

'Just don't,' he said anxiously, 'let her get anywhere near the studio.'

In the morning, Fanny did not wake up. She lay curled in foetal position and only whimpered restlessly, drawing the covers over her head, when Zita called her name softly.

'It's the five-hour time difference,' David said know-ledgeably. 'Catching up with her. She won't surface until some time this afternoon.'

Zita felt a pang, because he knew so much about it, and because it was nearly time for him to leave for the airport. Cursing Caroline for thrusting the un-wanted responsibility upon her, Zita cast an anguished glance upstairs. 'I wanted to go to the airport with you,' she mourned.

'Hopeless, love,' he said. 'It would take too long – and only prolong the agony.'

She gave him a heartfelt look, and he relented slightly. 'Tell you what,' he temporized, 'we'll split the difference.' He, too, glanced upwards towards the guest-room. 'She should sleep a while yet. You can come with me to the Air Terminal at Victoria. Then you ought to get back here well before she wakes up. In case she does, you can leave a note.' He hesitated. 'She *can* read?'

'I should hope so.' Zita fought down an impulse to laugh. 'She's nine years old.'

'You can't tell,' he said darkly, defensively. 'She's been educated in California. She was pretty hopeless when I knew her. And she doesn't seem to have im-proved much.'

'Never mind.' Zita brushed this aside, the desire for another couple of hours with David warring and winning over her instinct to remain with Fanny. 'Let's leave a note and risk it.'

David pulled her to him, gratefully and kissed her.

She tried not to think of Caroline.

'You write the note,' he said. 'I'll get a taxi.'

It was over too soon: the taxi ride . . . the checking in . . . the nervous, chattering, time-filling wait until the announcement over the Tannoy . . .

'You'll write?' Zita gasped.

'I'll phone,' David swore.

And then, inexorably, the passengers presented their cards and filed down the ramp into the waiting bus, like some new breed of Cretan about to be sacrificed to the latest Minotaur – a monster who would spread his fickle wings and carry them off. Perhaps to deliver them safely on some strange shore, or perhaps to devour them in one greedy gulp of noise and flame.

Perhaps the waiting – the fear of the final decision – was worst of all for those left behind.

A taxi was too much of an extravagance twice in one day. After the last long lingering kiss, Zita tried to turn her brain off as she made her way to the Tube and the Angel. She was almost successful.

Only in some deep vestigial remnant of her consciousness was there the vague sensation that she was being followed.

There was a strong smell of burning as she opened the front door. 'Fanny! Are you there?' she called out. 'What's going on?'

'I'm making breakfast.' The small, determined figure

appeared at the end of the hall. 'But this stupid bacon won't cook right. It's too thick.'

Zita pulled off her coat and hurried into the kitchen. At first glance, the debris was everywhere. It took a moment of quiet deep breathing before the damage sorted itself into manageable form. It was the haze of acrid smoke hanging in the air which made the situation seem so desperate. Some of it was coming from the sizzling snarling frying pan on the gas stove, but most of it was thinning out from the thick black plume arising from the electric toaster.

Zita dashed to the table, turned the toaster off, and flipped both sides open. Two charred chunks of ill-cut bread slid away from the electric coils.

'You mean it doesn't pop up by itself?' Fanny asked in amazement. 'Gee, this whole place is really out of the Ark, isn't it? How do you stand living like this?'

'Very well – usually,' Zita said, between clenched teeth. She turned the gas jet off and lifted the frying pan just as the grease was about to catch alight. She drained it into the waste tin and looked at the shrivelled remains of the bacon.

There had been only one egg left. She saw that Fanny had managed to drop that in the sink. A rapidly-drying streak of yellow trailed from a crushed shell in the middle of the sink to the drain.

'I was hungry,' Fanny said defensively. 'Anyhow, your letter said to make myself at home. I only wanted breakfast.'

'In any case – ' Zita tried to be calm – and fair. She *had* left Fanny unattended, with just a vaguely welcoming note to salve her conscience – 'it's tea-time now. Why don't I make tea for us both, instead?'

'Okay,' Fanny said reluctantly. 'But I'd rather have a glass of milk.'

'All right.' Zita couldn't help smiling. 'You can have a glass of milk for tea.'

'But – ' All the events of the previous day, the time difference, the strangeness of everything in this strange country, seemed to bear down on Fanny at once, slumping her shoulders and bowing her head.

'Okay, thanks,' she said, looking as close to defeated as, perhaps, she might ever look.

'And listen – ' she looked up, tossing her head back – 'I'm sorry. I didn't *mean* to make such a mess. It just . . . happened. Everything got away from me, like.'

'It's all right,' Zita said. 'I expect I'd be lost in one of your American kitchens.'

It restored Fanny's spirit – perhaps too much. She levelled a thoughtful gaze at Zita. 'Yeah, I expect you would,' she said. 'I bet you'd blow the joint up. At least I didn't do that.'

After tea, Fanny was fretful. She declined an invitation to take a walk exploring the neighbourhood with an expression bordering on disgust. She constantly flipped over the channels of the television set, incredulous that so few programmes were available. She listened briefly to the radio, once again flipping through stations, searching for something that might be familiar to her.

In one way, Zita sympathized; in another way, she

found this behaviour extremely tiresome. Her efforts at conversation were, it seemed, as dull as anything on radio or television. She reminded herself again that Fanny had been callously deserted by her mother – it was no wonder the child was edgy and upset.

Indicating the bookcases and magazine rack, Zita abandoned any further attempts to talk to Fanny. Very shortly after, however, she found Fanny dogging her footsteps as she went about her long-delayed house-work. Several times, Fanny seemed about to say some-thing. Each time, she changed her mind and turned away. In the end, Zita resigned herself to the small, silent, somehow accusing presence tagging behind and nearly forgot her.

She wondered if David's plane had left on time. If it had good safe engines, if the landing gear was retracting properly, if the fuel lines were unclogged, if the pilot and co-pilot were in good health and had had enough sleep last night, if there were any hi-jackers aboard, if David would remember to call her immediately from New York, as soon as he landed safely – if he landed safely . . . Oh, there was more to worry about in the world than Fanny's little problems.

Fanny snapped out of her doldrums briefly when the evening newspaper popped through the mail slot. She snatched it from the door and retreated to a corner of the living-room with it, rustling the pages intently. After some moments of peace, Zita looked up from her ironing to find Fanny in front of her again, re-garding her intently.

'Can we go to a movie?' Fanny asked.

'Perhaps,' Zita said cautiously. 'Which one would you like to see?'

'It's okay – it's local,' Fanny said. 'I checked. It starts in half an hour. So, can we go?'

It was the first time in hours that Fanny had shown any signs of animation, but an uneasy suspicion of the local programme shadowed Zita's memory. 'We'll see,' she said.

'Oh . . . please,' Fanny coaxed. The word sounded foreign coming from her, it was obviously one she had never used much.

'Let me check the programme.' Zita took the newspaper, already turned to the entertainments page.

'It's a swell double feature,' Fanny said enthusiastically. 'It really is. It's *Blood Bath On Mars* and *The Return of the Mad Monster*.'

'I'm sorry.' Zita had found the advertisement. 'I'm afraid we can't.'

'It's all right,' Fanny said grandly. 'I've got my own money. I'll even take you.'

'We can't,' Zita said. 'They're both X Certificate. They wouldn't let you in.'

'You're crazy,' Fanny said. 'I told you – I've got my own money.'

'You don't understand,' Zita said. 'Both films are X Certificates. Children aren't admitted.'

'But –' Fanny fought to comprehend. 'What about the matinee tomorrow, then? Can I go to that?'

'Yes, I should think so,' Zita said, 'but you won't see those films.'

'But why – it's the children's matinee, isn't it?'

'That's why. No one under the age of 18 can be admitted to an X-Certificate film.'

'I've got my own money.' Fanny clung desperately to the only standard she knew. 'I can pay. If I've got the money, they've *got* to let me in.'

'They can't let you in – they'd be breaking the law if they did. I'm afraid you can't go to that cinema. Not while that programme is playing.'

'What kind of stupid law is that?' Fanny screamed, tears and temper surfacing together.

'It's English law,' Zita said quietly.

'It's a stupid law!' Fanny stamped her foot. 'We see those kind of movies all the time at home. They have them on television. All the kids in my school watch them every night. We watch them and laugh.'

'Well, you'll have to wait until you get home before you see them again,' Zita said.

'Yeah? Maybe I'm never going – ' Fanny broke off, looking frightened. As though she had said more than she had intended.

'Never *what?*' Zita snapped. But Fanny had dissolved into tears, and just shook her head. Zita tried to dismiss the uneasy feeling that Fanny might have reason to suspect that she was remaining permanently in England. Certainly, the child was too near hysterics for further questioning this evening.

'You're overtired,' she said. 'You've had a hard day. Why don't you go to bed early?'

Fanny shook her head. 'Don't want to,' she muttered.

Zita ignored this. 'First, you can have a nice cup of

cocoa and a scrambled egg,' she said enticingly. 'Then you can have a nice hot bath and use my foaming bath oil. Then you can just lie down and rest for a little while, even if you don't go to sleep. You can – '

She broke off, knowing that she had won. Still snuffling, Fanny had pulled out a chair, sitting down at the kitchen table and reaching for the box of cocoa.

Upstairs, drawing the shades in Fanny's room, Zita had a clear view of the square below.

The lamplights were just going on. At one corner of the square, a vaguely familiar figure stood looking up at the house.

She must be imagining things; but, even as she drew the curtain, the figure ducked back, as though anxious to avoid being seen.

But she had seen him earlier that day. In those last moments after leaving David and before descending into the Tube, when she had had the disturbing sensation of being followed.

Now her follower was in the square below, watching her home.

CHAPTER IV

'WHAT'S THE MATTER?' Fanny asked sleepily from the bed.

'Nothing.' Zita jerked the curtains closed and turned away from the window sharply. 'Do you want the night light left on?'

'I'm not a baby.' Fanny's eyes drooped heavily, she snuggled down into the pillow. 'Besides, it isn't even dark out yet. Not real dark. Doesn't it ever get real dark here? Every time I wake up, it's light out.'

'It will be dark soon,' Zita soothed. 'Just go to sleep.'

It was, of course, a fatal remark to make. Fanny sat up abruptly.

'Where's Romeo?' she demanded. 'Where is he?'

'Who on earth – ?'

'There he is.' Fanny pointed imperiously to the suede giraffe, sprawling on top of the dresser. 'Bring him here!' The urgency in her voice outweighed any other considerations. Fanny did not mean to be rude; she was a child, in a strange situation, in a strange country. She wanted her new toy – something of her own to cling to.

'So you've decided on his name.' Zita brought the doll over to the bed.

'Yeah.' Fanny reached for it hungrily. 'And I'm gonna get another one just like it, and I'll name it – '

'Juliet?' Zita offered.

'Naw!' Fanny gave her a look of flat amazement. 'I'll name him Alfa. Who ever heard of a car called Juliet-Romeo?'

Zita choked back a sudden burst of amusement. Downstairs, the phone rang suddenly. David –

Fanny sat up and began to get out of bed. 'Maybe it's Caroline,' she said.

'Get back in bed!' Zita snapped. She *could* not have her conversation with David monitored by Fanny.

'But – '

'It couldn't possibly be Caroline,' Zita said. 'She's on a ship somewhere.'

'Oh, yeah.' Fanny drew her legs back under the covers, a wary expression flickered across her face. 'I forgot.' She flung herself back against the pillows, screwing her eyes up in an improbable imitation of instant slumber.

Zita looked at her uneasily, but downstairs the telephone kept ringing urgently. She closed Fanny's door firmly and hurried downstairs.

The phone stopped ringing just as she lifted the receiver. 'Hello – ' she said desperately. 'Hello – ' Willing an answer from the Transatlantic Operator, but there was none. The ridiculous contretemps with Fanny had cost her David's call. She slammed down the receiver in exasperation and stood there, hopefully waiting for it to ring again.

It was silent. She moved to the sofa and sat down, picking up a magazine. It must ring again, at any moment. How long would David wait before trying again. Fifteen minutes? Half an hour? An hour?

A floorboard creaked overhead, then another. Fanny was on the prowl.

Zita flung the magazine aside and stood up. Looking up from the foot of the stairs, she could see Fanny's door ajar and the glimmer of a white nightie where Fanny stood silently listening.

'Go back to bed, Fanny,' Zita called. There was no response, nor had she expected one. She, too, waited silently. After long minutes, the door at the head of the stairs closed quietly and the floorboards creaked again as Fanny tiptoed back to bed . . .

The telephone did not ring again. Zita watched the Late News, comforting herself with the dubious thought that, had the plane crashed, the newsflash would certainly have been on at the end of the programme. So David must be all right. He was either too tired, or too tied up with his business contacts to ring again tonight. Also, he would be mindful of the time difference and not want to disturb her at too late an hour. She might as well go to bed.

She wrote a note: '2 extra pints, please, until further notice' and put out the milk bottles. Straightening, she looked out across the square. It was deserted now, no sign of the American tourist who had been lurking there earlier; probably not even noticing the house, but waiting to get the right combination of light and shadow for his camera.

Turning back into the house and bolting the door behind her, she wondered just when her subconscious had come to the conclusion that he had been American. The tourist part was easy – the camera automatically brought that idea to mind. But American? Partly, it was the impression of close-cropped hair, and partly the chunky, solid set of his body, faintly reminiscent of someone familiar to her. Or just generally familiar because of all the American tourists she had encountered around Camden Passage?

Too late, now, to be bothered about it. He had gone. And she was tired. Yawning, she turned out the lights and climbed the stairs.

The sound of rain beat through her dreams as she drifted back to consciousness, bringing with it a sense of depression she was still too sleepy to analyse. She usually didn't mind rainy days.

Downstairs, the telephone rang twice – and stopped.

'David!' It jolted her into full wakefulness and she groped for her robe. But the phone had stopped ringing. She blinked at her watch: eight o'clock. That meant it was somewhere about 3.00 a.m. in New York. Unlikely to be David, then.

Unlikely to be David for several more hours, in fact. The weight of depression settled on her more heavily. No David, no news, rain pelting down outside – and Fanny the Fiend to try to entertain. It was pretty much a certainty that Fanny, accustomed to sunny Californian days, was not going to be enchanted by a wet London morning.

Opening the bedroom door, she heard Fanny's voice, but could not distinguish any words. Had Fanny answered the phone?

'Fanny?' she called, starting down the stairs. 'Fanny, who is it?'

'Nobody,' Fanny shouted. There was another indistinguishable murmur and Fanny slammed down the receiver as Zita appeared in the doorway.

'It was a wrong number,' she said. Her eyes slid guiltily to the portrait of Caroline over the mantel.

'You were talking a long time for a wrong number.' Zita tried to assure herself that her sudden suspicion that Fanny had been talking to Caroline was unfounded. Caroline was somewhere at sea in Xavier's yacht. But some yachts had ship-to-shore communication and, judging from certain veiled references in some newspapers, Xavier was always in a position to communicate with his business interests – whatever they might be.

'I couldn't understand what they wanted, right away,' Fanny said. 'They talked all funny. Worse than you, even.'

Zita ignored the dubious plural, as she ignored the slur on her English accent. Fanny was lying, but there was nothing to be gained by making her admit it.

'Are you going to eat now?' Fanny moved away from the phone, glancing again at Caroline's portrait. 'I'm not very hungry.' She yawned, suddenly appealingly childlike in the unguarded moment.

Perhaps, after all, Fanny had been *pretending* to talk on the telephone, holding the receiver while she spoke to the portrait of the mother who had so casually abandoned her.

'You can have a glass of milk,' Zita said. 'You needn't have anything else, unless you want to.' For Fanny, too, it must seem like 3.00 a.m., or even earlier. Wasn't there an additional time difference between New York and California? Fanny was dislocated out of any familiar pattern – time, family or country. No wonder she was upset and disoriented.

Three pints of milk on the doorstep and – a quick glance around – no strangers in the square. Zita closed the front door thankfully, more relieved than she liked to admit to herself. The emptiness of the square was not surprising. In this downpour, the presence of a stray tourist would have been particularly disturbing. Even more so than one last night. Perhaps she had grown unaccustomed to living alone during this past year of marriage. The mere knowledge that David was no longer at hand to turn to had her building sinister phantoms out of something that quite probably had an innocent explanation, could she but know it.

'I'll help.' Fanny took one of the bottles. 'Aren't these tiny? *We* always get half-gallon cartons.'

'Good for you,' Zita said, wishing she could tell Fanny to go and get dressed. But Fanny had obviously been up for some time. She was wearing a faded striped tee-shirt and a pair of jeans that were slightly frayed at the cuffs. Incongruously, she still had the bulging handbag swinging from its shoulder strap at her side, obviously unwilling to relinquish whatever security it represented to her mind.

'What are we going to do today?' Fanny's challenge

was querulous, but not quite whining – not yet. 'Can we go to a movie today?'

She wasn't going to go through *that* again! 'Why don't we go sightseeing?' Zita suggested brightly. 'You haven't seen anything of London yet.'

'In this rain?' Fanny was incredulous.

'We don't,' Zita said firmly, 'allow a little thing like rain to stop us doing anything.'

'Yeah.' Fanny considered this a moment. 'Yeah, I guess, if you did, you'd never get anything done.'

The doorbell rang. Zita hurriedly put the milk bottles on the kitchen table and went back to the front door, Fanny trailing behind her.

A dark, gypsy-like man stood there, cap pulled well down over his eyes, holding a triangular ladder. Zita stared at him blankly, realizing she had expected a postboy bringing a cablegram from David.

'Wash your windows?'

'On a day like this?' Zita heard an echo of Fanny in her own voice.

'Uh . . . . no.' The man shifted the ladder uneasily. 'Take orders today, come back and clean later. That way, lose no time, see?'

But he was the one trying to see. He sidestepped slightly, craning his neck, trying to look into the hall-way behind Zita.

'No, thank you,' Zita said sharply. 'We have a regular cleaner.' Fanny tried to crowd forward and Zita pushed her back.

'Give cheap price. Do good job.' He moved again, staring over her shoulder. For an instant, she had the impression that he was about to try to force his way into the house.

She stepped back quickly, beginning to close the door. He transferred his attention to her, abruptly making her aware of her robe and slippers, her lack of make-up, emphasizing her vulnerable position – alone in the house, with a child under her care.

'I'm sorry, no.' She slammed the door, shooting home the supplementary bolt she rarely bothered to use, feeling shaken.

'Who was that?' Fanny asked.

'I don't know,' Zita said, amending, 'a window cleaner. They come around sometimes.' But not very often. This was, in fact, the first one she had seen since they had engaged their regular cleaner.

'I'm going to get dressed,' she told Fanny, pulling herself together. 'Go and have a glass of milk. And don't – ' she called over the banister – 'don't let any-one in – '

'Don't – ' she insisted, to Fanny's retreating back – 'don't answer the door, if the bell rings.'

The Houses of Parliament were a washout, the National Gallery a dead loss. Zita suspected that the Tower of London, with its 'buckets of blood' routine, would be more up Fanny's street, but the pouring rain precluded this. They finished at Madame Tussaud's instead. Fanny lost some of her boredom in the Chamber of Horrors, but mourned her lack of knowledge of the more sinister of its inhabitants.

'You can study your guidebook,' Zita said. 'It will

tell you all about them.'

'And then I'll know, next time we come.' Fanny glanced complacently at the severed heads in the cobwebbed niches along the stairs. 'My father would be amazed if he knew where I was right now,' she said, with relish.

Again, there was a disturbing sense of double-meaning in Fanny's simple sentence. It tied up with something else that had been bothering Zita for some time.

'By the way,' she said casually. 'How did you manage to bring those cigarettes and drink through Customs? Surely they wouldn't be part of your allowance at your age.'

'Oh, it was easy,' Fanny said. 'Just like Caroline said it would be. I put them at the bottom of my bag and then I walked through beside a grown-up, so it would look like I was carrying it for them, if anybody found it. And Caroline was waiting for me. So they didn't look. They only looked at Caroline – men always do.'

That was indisputable. But, was the rest a bit too glib? Fanny had reeled the story off with scarcely a pause for breath. Because it was the truth – or because she had been carefully rehearsed in it? Zita was not at all reassured that Caroline had actually met Fanny at Heathrow. It seemed just as likely that she had flown all the way with her, brought her allowance in herself, and left Fanny at the airport while she met Zita for lunch and persuaded her to take care of Fanny for a few weeks. She recalled uneasily that the cigarettes Caroline had offered her at lunch had had a health warning printed on the packet – and export cigarettes don't carry one.

But why? Zita realized with despair that Caroline's way of thinking was too devious, too involved, for any ordinary mortal to follow. Only one thing was certain: Caroline *did* have a motive. One that doubtless seemed logical to her. No matter how roughshod she must ride over other people's feelings.

'It's too bad,' Zita said, with sudden sympathy, 'that you've come all this way, and then your mother – '

'Oh, that's all right,' Fanny said airily. 'You're not so bad. And besides, it will only be for a little while. And then we'll be together for always. Caroline promised.'

Caroline had promised a lot of things in her time. Including 'to love, honour and cherish . . . until death do us part' – on several occasions. But that brought David back into the picture – and clouded the picture. And Zita didn't want to do that.

Because a picture *was* slowly emerging. From an idea, here; a fragment of a sentence, there; a general knowledge of Caroline's methods and complete irresponsibility –

'Wouldn't you rather have gone to India with your father?' Zita asked.

'India – ?' Fanny's face was a total blank for a moment, but she recovered quickly. 'Oh, I don't know. It's probably lousy there. Maybe I'll go later – after they've got a house, and everything.'

'I see,' Zita said grimly. Once again, Fanny had been

too glib, too facile with her explanation. Or her cover-up.

'It's time to be getting home now,' Zita said. Ignoring Fanny's protest, she marched her relentlessly toward Baker Street Tube Station. She bought tickets for the Angel, and was not surprised that a vaguely familiar figure picked up their trail as they emerged from the Angel and followed them back to the house in the square.

Because it all made sense – in its own strange way. Once you began to get an insight into Caroline's convoluted character, if not to understand her, it became simple.

You had only to ask yourself: *What would be the most awful, useless, idiotic, completely irresponsible thing Caroline could do?* And the answer came back, loud and clear: *Kidnap her own child.*

Not only that but, having kidnapped her, park her with someone else until the fuss died down. Leave her little cuckoo in the nest of an ex-husband and his wife – while Caroline herself took off on a Mediterranean cruise, either to give herself an alibi, or because the opportunity had suddenly arisen and it sounded more glamorous than staying at home taking care of a child.

No wonder a rather forlorn little man was trailing them around town and lurking in the square. As she opened the front door, Zita resisted an impulse to turn around and call out, *'Here she is. Come and take her.'* Because you really couldn't do a thing like that. For

Fanny's sake, if not for Caroline's, the matter must be more delicately handled.

Closing the door behind them, and once more slamming home the supplementary bolt, Zita determined that she would end this situation as soon as decently possible. Now that Fanny's father knew where Fanny was located, he would surely go to the police for assistance. Or perhaps he would simply come to the door himself and explain the problem face-to-face. It would depend, of course, on whether he thought David and Zita were Caroline's willing helpers, or simply her dupes.

Whatever happened, Zita decided, she would have no part in the pointless game of International Tug o' War, which sometimes developed around the unfortunate children of divorce. At the first decent opportunity, she would relinquish Fanny into the custody of her rightful guardian. And Caroline could go to –

The telephone rang. Fanny dashed to answer it, but Zita's legs were longer and she beat her by several yards, catching up the receiver with a childish thrill of achievement.

'Hello?' Zita said breathlessly. 'Hello?'

Her immediate hopes were dashed. A series of pips ruled out the possibility of an Overseas call. (Where *was* David? *What* was he doing? He had *promised* to call.) A coin rang into a slot and the pips ceased. Zita drew a steadying breath.

'David Falbridge Studio,' she announced primly. 'Good afternoon.'

There was no answer. Zita repeated her statement,

a little more briskly. At the other end of the line, she could hear someone breathing.

'This is the David Falbridge Studio,' Zita said again. 'What number are you calling?'

There was a sharp click, and the dial tone buzzed in Zita's ear. She replaced the receiver carefully and met Fanny's eyes. It was suddenly important not to alarm the child.

'It must have been another wrong number,' she said.

Fanny stared at her accusingly. 'You should have let *me* answer.'

CHAPTER V

NEXT MORNING was grey, but dry. Later, the sun might even come out. Zita felt a sense of accomplishment at being awake and up before Fanny. She enjoyed the luxury of a solitary breakfast, reading the newspaper over her coffee. It was even rather luxurious to be able to Hoover the carpet without dodging around small feet. Of course, one's own children would be much better brought up, but –

'Hi.' Fanny stood in the doorway, her wiry little frame again in the faded tee-shirt and jeans. She carried Romeo on one arm, her handbag on the other. As Zita looked at her, she hugged the handbag tighter.

'Can we go to the movies today?' she asked, but some of the old fire was missing. She sounded strangely defensive. 'It's still an X-Certificate programme,' Zita said automatically, a newly-stirring maternal instinct prompting immediate suspicions. The question was a try-on. Fanny had not really expected the answer to change. Therefore, she wanted to put Zita in the wrong, in the hope that Zita would be annoyed enough, or distracted enough, not to notice – what?

'Can I have some breakfast?' Fanny shifted uneasily under Zita's steady gaze. In doing so, she turned slightly, exposing another view of Romeo's long spotted fawn suede neck. A thin line of crimson streaked across the neck, a blob of cerulean extended from the end of a dark brown suede spot. 'I'm awfully hungry.'

'You've been in the studio!' Zita accused.

'No, I haven't.' Fanny backed away.

Without answering, Zita rushed past her and up the stairs. David had locked the studio door and given her the key, which she had hidden in the corner of her own jewel box. How could Fanny have – ?

The door leading to the stairs to the studio stood ajar, a key protruding from the lock. Zita dashed up the final flight of stairs and into the studio.

'I never touched anything.' Fanny stumbled up the stairs behind her. 'I only wanted to look.'

At first glance, the studio seemed undisturbed. The stack of canvasses still rested face against the wall. The easel in the centre of the room still bore the unfinished canvas David had shrouded with an old paint rag to await his return. On the table beside it, paints gleamed wetly on his pallette.

Fanny twitched unhappily as Zita's gaze rested on the shrouded canvas and did not move away. 'There's nothing up here, anyway,' she said. 'I thought there was something exciting, because the door was locked, but – '

'That's another thing,' Zita said slowly. 'The door *was* locked. You took the key from my room. You were going through my jewel box.' There was nothing of any great value in it, a few bits and pieces with garnets and seed pearls inherited from her grandmother, but it was the principle of the thing.

'I never!' Fanny said wildly. 'I never did! That's a dirty lie!'

'*And* you've touched things here.' The meaning of the wet paints registered. Zita walked over and twitched aside the paint rag.

A jagged slash of crimson swept through the sky from the top of the painting to the line of roofs in the foreground, like red lightning hitting one of the houses. Two white clouds had been outlined in cerulean. It had often been said that David's painting didn't need a signature. Certainly, it didn't need Fanny's signature.

She swung to face Fanny accusingly. Fanny stood her ground – sullen, mutinous, ready to go down fighting. 'I *never* touched your jewel box,' she said.

'You told me you didn't touch anything up here, either.' Zita gestured toward the canvas. 'How do you explain that?'

'That doesn't count,' Fanny said. 'Old Stupid can fix it, easy. It was just a joke on him.'

Actually, David *could* fix it. She could probably fix it herself. The paint on the canvas was a few days old and moderately dry. Fanny's additions could be removed, or lessened, by a little careful cleaning.

But that was not the point. The point was that Fanny was going to be in this house for another two and a half weeks. Perhaps longer, if Caroline didn't feel like facing up to her responsibilities. The point was that Fanny could not be allowed to run wild through the house, doing exactly as she pleased. It was, in fact, a question of just *who* was going to be in command for the length of Fanny's visit.

'Go to your room,' Zita said, with dangerous quiet. 'Go to your room – and stay there.'

'I won't.' Fanny began backing away. 'You can't make me. You can't tell me what to do – you're not my mother.'

'Your mother isn't here,' Zita said. 'I am.'

Fanny halted and advanced a step, unleashing what she evidently took to be her most potent threat. 'I'll tell Caroline on you!'

'You're perfectly at liberty to,' Zita said. 'There are a few things I intend to tell Caroline myself. Now – go to your room!'

Fanny wavered, turned, and turned back. 'I hate you!' she howled suddenly. 'You're mean and nasty and awful! No wonder Old Stupid still has Caroline's picture hanging up. He wouldn't want a picture of *you* on the wall!'

She hadn't intended to do it. She hadn't realized that she would do it. Of its own volition, Zita's hand suddenly lashed out and boxed Fanny's ear.

They stared at each other, almost mutually aghast. But Fanny couldn't know that it had been sheer reflex action. In the war of nerves, Fanny's nerve snapped.

'Yaaah!' she wailed, turning and bolting down the stairs. 'Yaaah!' The slam of her bedroom door punctuated the yowls, after which they subsided into a steady monotonous sobbing, which eventually lessened into brooding silence.

Later, she would make peace with Fanny, but first she must gain control of herself. She was still shaking with the anger Fanny's shot had triggered off. Zita

took several deep breaths. She would not think of
Fanny right now. Neither would she think of Caroline
– and David.

She would, for the moment, try to concentrate on
repairing the damage that had been done. She opened
a bottle of turpentine, moistened the paint rag and,
with feather-light strokes, gently began to remove
Fanny's overpainting from David's canvas.

Less than an hour had passed when she became conscious of the strangely empty feeling to the house.
There had been no whimper from Fanny for ages and,
absorbed in her delicate task, she had nearly forgotten
her. Now, she could remove no more of the daubed
paint without also removing the work beneath it.
David would have to finish the task himself, and re-
paint where necessary. He would not be pleased – he
had specifically warned her to keep Fanny away from
the studio.

Laying aside the paint rag and restoppering the
bottle of turpentine, she paused. The silence of the
house caught at her like a tangible thing. Absurdly,
she had the conviction that she was alone in the house.
Shaken, she covered the painting again and went downstairs to investigate. She did not bother to lock the
door at the foot of the stairs. Fanny had learned her
lesson – she would not venture into the studio again.
In any case, locks seemed a challenge to her rather
than a deterrent.

She tapped on the closed bedroom door. 'Fanny?'
she called. 'Fanny?'

She had not really expected an answer. She turned the knob and the door opened. At least Fanny had not locked herself in. Again, she was conscious of a desolate empty feeling as she stepped into the room.

Fanny was gone. She checked the closet: Fanny's coat was gone, too.

There wasn't much doubt but, automatically, Zita went through the rest of the house. It was empty. Fanny had run away.

Zita made a cup of coffee and carried it into the living-room, where she sat down and considered the position. There was no point in panicking – that was undoubtedly just what Fanny hoped she would do. Nothing would please Fanny better than to stroll in casually after a couple of hours and find an hysterical hostess and police all over the place.

Apart from which, there was an additional objection to calling in the police: Fanny's father.

Had Fanny, in fact, run away? Or had she looked out of the window and seen her father beckoning to her? In which case, it was not surprising that she should dash out of the house without stopping to say anything.

She had not taken her cases with her, so she must have expected to return. Whether her father would allow her to come back to collect her cases, or even to say goodbye, was another matter. Her father could not really be blamed if he had formed the opinion that Zita and David were Caroline's willing allies. Naturally, he would not wish Fanny to come near the house again. And replacing an abandoned wardrobe would represent no problem to a doting American daddy.

The coffee had grown cold. Zita stared at it absently. On the other hand, Fanny might simply have decided to try to find the cinema by herself and gain admittance. She had taken her bag and had plenty of money. (More, Zita suspected, than her own monthly housekeeping allowance.)

Again, in that case, there was no need to notify the police. It was necessary to do nothing but wait for Fanny to decide to return of her own accord. But waiting was the hardest thing of all to do.

She glanced at her watch. Half past two. The sensible thing would be to go out into the kitchen and have some lunch. Fanny, she was sure, would have bought herself a good meal somewhere. Or would have one bought for her.

Zita got up and crossed to the window, looking out on the square. It was deserted. Nor had the doorbell or telephone rung all day.

No one had any interest in this house any more – now that Fanny was no longer in it.

By quarter to five, she admitted to herself that Fanny was the winner in this particular battle of nerves. If she hadn't heard anything by nightfall, she would *have* to call in the police. One couldn't leave a small child – no matter how precocious – to roam through a strange city in what was, to the child, a foreign country. Neither could one blithely assume that the child was safely with her father.

If something were wrong, Zita would never forgive herself. However spiteful Fanny's intentions, she was still a child. She might have been struck by a car while crossing the street, forgetful that traffic went in the opposite direction here –

No, Zita determined, she could not wait very much longer before calling the police – perhaps not even until darkness. Undoubtedly, Caroline would be furious – when she returned – to find that the police had been involved. But Caroline would just have to lump it!

The telephone shrilled abruptly and Zita pounced on it. The pips denoting a local call sounded in her ear, giving a curious reassurance, then the click and clunk of a coin being pushed home. A faint, familiar, childish voice said, 'Hello – ?'

Relief and fury exploded in equal proportions. 'Fanny, I'm very angry with you,' Zita snapped. 'Come back here at once – you can find your own way. I have no intention of coming to get you. You can take a taxi. You had no right to leave the house without my permission –'

'Oooh!' A choking gasp cut her off in mid-sentence. 'Fanny! Where's Fanny?' The voice was high, shrill, still childlike – but now unmistakably Caroline's.

'I do not know where Fanny is.' Zita spaced her words out with deadly intensity, her fury turning from Fanny to Caroline – where – in all honesty – it belonged. If it were not for Caroline, none of them would be in this predicament.

'What do you mean – you don't know?' Caroline

shrilled indignantly. 'You were taking care of her. I *trusted* her to you.'

'Perhaps you should have explained that to her. She didn't seem to want to stay here. Quite frankly, she behaved abominably. And then she ran away.'

'She can't have,' Caroline wailed. 'She'll ruin everything. Where did she go?'

'If I knew that,' Zita pointed out reasonably, 'I couldn't have said she'd run away. I'd have been able to say where she had gone.'

'But you *must* have some idea,' Caroline said. 'She can't have just – gone.'

'I'm afraid that's just what she did,' Zita said. 'As a matter of fact, I was just about to call the police.'

'No – ' Caroline choked. 'No – don't!'

'Why not?' Zita felt relief, rather than surprise. Caroline's instant reaction seemed to prove her theory.

'Because – Because – You can't – ' Caroline floundered. 'She's just a child. It would be too awful to have the police after her – hunting her. It would frighten her.'

'She might be even more frightened,' Zita pointed out, 'lost and alone in a strange city. She might be very glad to see the police.'

'No!' Again, the protest was swift and immediate, as though forced involuntarily from Caroline's throat. 'No. She'll be all right. She's a very . . . self-sufficient . . . child. It – it would do something dreadful to her psychologically, I'm sure. Give her traumas, or something.'

The idea certainly seemed to be giving Caroline

traumas, Zita thought with grim amusement.

'All right.' She stopped toying with Caroline. 'You needn't keep this up any longer. I know where she is, just as well as you do. She's with her father.'

'Her father?' If she hadn't know Caroline to be such a practised liar, Zita would have sworn the amazement in her voice was genuine.

'That's right,' Zita said coldly. 'Her father. He's turned up and snatched her back – and the best of British luck to him.'

'What *are* you talking about?' Caroline's bewilderment began to force unwilling belief. 'Jeff's gone to India. He couldn't possibly have taken Fanny. He hasn't even taken his sons with him – not until he's found a house and got settled. Then he's going to send for the children.'

'But – ' Now it was Zita floundering in waters out of her depth. 'He must have. He's been watching the house, following us. I've seen him. A medium-sized, rather stocky man, with a crew cut and camera – '

'That proves it!' Caroline said triumphantly. 'Jeff is *very* tall and thin – and he wouldn't *dream* of having a crew cut. And he never *could* work a camera!'

Even liars must tell the truth occasionally. Something in Caroline's very righteousness commanded belief.

'But . . . who was he, then?' Zita asked weakly. 'He *was* watching the house. And where *is* Fanny? Good Lord – we've *got* to report this to the police. Immediately!'

'No, no.' The maddeningly evasive note was back in

Caroline's voice as she tried to be soothing. 'Fanny will be all right. There's no need to drag the police into this. We can just get her back ourselves.'

'Get her back ourselves?'

'Of course,' Caroline said. 'I expect you to help me. It's the least you can do. After all, I left Fanny in your care, and you went and let this happen. You *owe* it to poor little Fanny.'

'Poor little Fanny?' Zita's brain reeled, as much from Caroline's logic, as from her description of the child David had so much more fittingly described as Fanny the Fiend.

'I'm glad you see it my way,' Caroline said severely. 'Now, if we move quickly, we ought to get this whole thing sorted out by morning. Not that that isn't too long a time for poor little Fanny to have been upset. Really, I don't see how you could have been so careless.'

Zita swallowed. There was no point in arguing with Caroline at this stage. In a way, she even agreed with her – she *should* have kept better watch over Fanny. If only because Fanny was Caroline's child and Caroline had seemed to abandon her – and nothing Caroline ever did was as simple as it seemed.

'How do you suggest we go about it?' Zita asked. 'Do *you* know where Fanny is?'

'How on earth could I know a thing like that?' Caroline sidestepped blandly. 'But I might just know somebody who might be able to tell us something,' she added disquietingly. 'You'll have to meet me at Reading and we'll go on from there.'

'Reading?' Zita had the dizzy sensation any conversation with Caroline inevitably brought on.

'Reading, Berkshire,' Caroline said. 'There are frequent trains from Paddington. If you leave right now, you ought to be able to get one within the hour. I'll meet you at Reading.'

'Reading,' Zita repeated faintly, knowing she was already condemned to this course of action.

'That's right,' Caroline said. 'And,' she added witheringly, 'please make sure that you're not being followed *this* time.'

CHAPTER VI

As she handed in her ticket at Reading, all Zita's misgivings crystallized. Perhaps she should have bought a return ticket. Perhaps she should never have left the house at all. As usual, Caroline had rushed her into a situation before she had had time to consider it. The urgency in Caroline's voice, the impression she gave of having no one else to turn to – But there was no point in trying to analyse the manner in which Caroline managed to get her own way. The fact was that Zita was here.

And Caroline wasn't. The other disembarking passengers had scattered, the train had pulled out again. When there had been no sign of Caroline inside the station, Zita had merely assumed that she had not wanted to buy a platform ticket – it was just the sort of maddening economy Caroline sometimes affected when she had been overextravagant in other ways. But she was not waiting outside the station, either.

At least – Zita looked around, with increasing bitterness, at the few unfamiliar faces passing by – she could be sure that she had not been followed. She had never seen any of these people before. Nor were any of them loitering. Everyone walked past with a firm determined step, obviously with a home to go to and on their way to that home. She wished the same could be said for herself.

It had been madness to allow Caroline to inveigle her into joining whatever wild goose chase was ahead. A kidnapping was a kidnapping – and the police were the proper people to handle it. She would make this clear to Caroline when Caroline deigned to show up. *If* Caroline deigned to show up.

It was growing dark, with the black lowering clouds of an impending storm. Zita wondered if Fanny were afraid of lightning . . . if she were terrified of her captors . . . if she had been given anything to eat. She had missed breakfast –

On the other hand, Zita abruptly checked the rush of guilt she felt at remembering the way she had disregarded Fanny's plea for food in order to track down the mischief she had done, Fanny might even now be sitting down to an excellent meal at the Ritz. Quite probably, with Caroline. Who else could have taken her away so smoothly? Caroline's telephone call to discover Fanny missing had been quite providentially timed. *And* had resulted in Zita's travelling miles out of the city. Had *that* been the real purpose of the call?

And yet, there *had* been someone lurking in the square, watching the house. Had it been to draw him away from the house that Caroline had insisted she come to Berkshire? When one was actually speaking to Caroline, her ideas seemed almost reasonable – if never admirable. It was later, when one began to think things over, that the credibility gap set in and widened rapidly.

You've got egg on your face. Zita smiled faintly as

Fanny's words returned to her. Fanny certainly had her mother taped – perhaps better than most adults Caroline came into contact with. It was probably as well for her that she had, if a little sad. It did not seem right that a child so young should be so disillusioned with the world already.

A low snarl of thunder rumbled in the distance. Zita decided that, if Caroline didn't arrive ahead of the storm, she would get the next train back to London. Once there, she would go immediately to the police – No, first home, to see if Fanny had, by any chance, come back. Or whether someone had called and removed Fanny's cases while the house was empty . . .

'*There* you are,' Caroline said accusingly from behind her, making it sound as though *she* had been the one waiting outside the station for over half an hour.

'There *you* are – ' Zita whirled around, but her feeble attempt to put the blame where it belonged trailed off into stunned silence.

Had she not heard the unmistakable voice, she would not have believed she was facing Caroline. The shimmering gilt hair she had been watching for subconsciously was hidden under a dingy cotton bandana. Dark, wraparound sunglasses shuttered those memorable violet eyes, hiding any expression and, curiously, drawing attention to the thin tracery of frown lines usually unnoticed on her forehead.

'Come along,' Caroline said crossly, she was frowning now. 'We can't stand here all night. It's going to rain.' She swung away, striding rapidly down the street, not turning to see if Zita was following.

Zita stood for a moment, still stunned, staring after her. She had never realized it before, but if anyone had ever asked her what the most unbelievable sight in her world would be, the answer would have been, *'Caroline, looking scruffy.'*

But Caroline looked scruffy now. Scruffy and non-descript. She wore a dark shapeless sweater and faded blue jeans – not even fashionable flared trousers – plain jeans. Slightly muddy tennis shoes completed the incredible outfit. Knowing herself for a cat, Zita still wished for a camera in her hands at that moment, so that she could preserve the sight for days when she herself was feeling scruffy. Or, better still, to prop the photograph on the mantel, beneath the hauntingly beautiful portrait.

Caroline was turning the corner, still without looking back. Zita snapped back to reality and put on a burst of speed that brought her abreast of Caroline. 'Where are we going?' she asked.

'The river,' Caroline said shortly. 'The boat is there.'

'But I thought – '

Caroline ignored her, striding ahead again. But surely a seagoing yacht could not sail this far up the Thames? And did Caroline really allow Xavier to see her looking like that? She must be more certain of him than anyone suspected. Or were they already married?

Caroline led the way through unfamiliar streets, turning finally on to the towpath beside the river. They walked past a dozen or so moored cabin cruisers, all curiously alike in name and paintwork, obviously hired pleasure boats. At the end boat, Caroline stopped.

'Here we are,' she said.

Zita stopped short as Caroline leaped nimbly aboard. This was no seagoing yacht, nor did it belong to Xavier. Not unless he had branched out into the hire-craft business. This was a small-size rented cabin cruiser, just about accommodating two.

The first enormous raindrops splattered on her face as she stood there, staring, and Caroline glanced back at her impatiently.

'Hurry up,' she said. 'You cast off, while I start the engine.'

More raindrops hurtled down with increasing intensity as Zita moved forward slowly. A sudden flash of lightning was followed almost immediately by a crash of thunder. The storm was upon them.

'Come *on*,' Caroline said. She took a deep breath and enunciated clearly. 'Untie the mooring rope from the iron ring and throw the rope aboard. Then come aboard yourself.'

'I know what "cast off" means,' Zita said indignantly.

'Then *do* it!' Caroline snapped. The engine choked, coughed, and throbbed into life. Zita stooped to untie the mooring rope, but the knot held against her efforts.

'Stop dallying!' Caroline showed every sign of developing into a Captain Bligh. 'We have another lock to get through – and they close them for the night.'

Zita tore at the knot in a fury and it gave way suddenly. She stood up, teetering slightly. The rope slipped down the river bank, which was rapidly turning to mud in the rain. The boat began to slide away from the shore.

'Jump!' Caroline shrieked. 'Hurry – jump!'

Skidding down the bank, Zita leaped desperately for the boat. Caroline clutched the wheel, fighting to keep the boat under control as it rocked wildly. 'Can't you be more careful?' she demanded, between clenched teeth.

'You told me to jump,' Zita said, moving forward to the overhanging shelter of the open wheelhouse. The rain turned into a steady downpour – heavy and depressing. 'Where are we going?'

'Upstream,' Caroline said. She glanced at Zita with annoyance. 'Haven't you brought anything with you?'

'Like what?' Boats didn't seem to bring out the better side of Caroline's nature. Zita was feeling a bit annoyed, herself.

'Pyjamas,' Caroline said, as though she ought to have known. 'A change of clothing. Something more suitable – trousers, or jeans.'

'You never mentioned such a thing,' Zita said. 'I didn't know I was expected to stay overnight – on a boat. I don't even know where we're going.'

'To get Fanny,' Caroline said grimly.

'Then you *do* know where she is!'

'She's all right,' Caroline said. 'Get into the cabin and change. I'll need you to help me at the next lock. You'll find another black sweater and a pair of jeans on my bunk. They ought to fit you well enough – you aren't *that* much bigger than me.'

Had she been less wet, Zita might have refused. But, however ungraciously Caroline worded the invitation, she had no option. Her suit jacket was soaking at the shoulders and back, where the downpour had drenched her while she stooped to untie the rope, and her hem slapped wet mud against the back of her legs. She stalked into the tiny forward cabin, childishly slamming the door.

Through the rain-curtained cabin windows, Zita watched the dripping landscape move lazily past as she changed. Caroline, she had to admit, handled the boat with a surprising adroitness.

The sweater was annoyingly clinging and the top button of the jeans refused to meet the buttonhole. After a short struggle, Zita let the sweater lap over it, hiding it. She hung her jacket and skirt, rather hopelessly, over the edge of the bunk to dry.

Caroline glanced up as the cabin door opened. 'Why don't you put the kettle on? We could use a cup of coffee.'

Well, it was an improvement over shouting orders, and she *could* use a cup of coffee. Zita filled the kettle, found the matches and lit the stove. Finding the instant coffee brought another interesting discovery: the galley shelves were completely stocked with tinned foods. Enough to allow anyone aboard to sit out a siege – or a three-week occupancy.

So much for the luxury cruise on Xavier's yacht which Caroline had claimed to be committed to. Why had she lied? Because it had seemed a more graceful way of fobbing off Fanny than just admitting that she didn't want a child around? Or because something had happened and she had not been invited on Xavier's cruise? Lying low and pretending that she was away on the cruise was just the sort of thing Caroline might do to save face among her friends.

In the wheelhouse, Caroline was staring ahead intently, trying to penetrate the lashing storm. Zita set a cup of coffee down beside the dark glasses on the ledge in front of the wheel. She carried her own coffee to the seat running along the inside of the hull and sat down within the shelter of the wheelhouse overhang. It put her in a position where she could see Caroline's face only in profile. But no one could ever tell anything from Caroline's expression, anyway.

The other boats had put in and were moored along the river banks. Although better with a boat than with a car, Caroline still didn't bother about other people's opinions. She pushed the boat ahead at close to full speed, not slowing as she passed the moored craft. Zita saw the boats tossing in their wake and occasionally glimpsed an angry face glaring after them from a cabin window. She did not suggest reducing speed, however. Caroline knew where she was going and, judging from her haste, the situation was rather more serious than she was admitting.

Not that Caroline ever admitted anything – not without a struggle. Zita sipped thoughtfully at her coffee and prepared to struggle.

'How is Xavier?' Zita asked abruptly.

'Xavier?' Caroline might never have heard the name before. But the boat yawed sharply and she spun the wheel back to return it to a straight course.

'I thought you were going on a cruise with him,' Zita persisted. 'To the Mediterranean. In his yacht.'

'Where on earth did you get an idea like that?' Caroline asked in amazement.

'As a matter of fact, you told me you were.'

'But I *couldn't* have.' Caroline turned the full force of wide, guileless violet eyes on Zita. 'It isn't true.'

At another time, it might have been funny. Caroline, acting as though she had ever possessed even a bowing acquaintance with truth. Acting was the word.

'I can see that,' Zita said. 'Nevertheless, it's what you told me.'

'You must have misunderstood.' Caroline turned her attention back to the river, just in time to make a crucial diversion to avoid a buoy. 'I must have said I was taking a short holiday on a boat, and you assumed I was going on a trip with Xavier. Everyone seems to think we're inseparable – it's all the fault of the newspapers. You can't believe everything you read in *them*.'

'I don't,' Zita said. Nevertheless, there are usually some indications of truth in most newspaper stories, and the stories concerning Xavier carried a nasty undercurrent of things left unsaid – libel laws being what they were.

'You probably read it in some gossip column,' Caroline conceded airily. 'It's just the sort of thing they *would* print.'

Caroline had decided upon her story and would obviously stick to it. Like all good liars, she seemed to have convinced herself of the utter truth of what she was saying. Unconcerned, except with the problem of steering, she frowned into the storm again, obviously feeling that the subject was closed, and everything had been explained satisfactorily.

'What *are* you doing on this boat?' Zita asked.

The cruiser veered sharply toward the shore, hesitated, and regained midstream. Caroline's face was placid as she turned slightly towards Zita and widened her eyes earnestly.

'Everything has been so hectic lately,' she said. 'I just felt that I needed some time to be alone . . . to be by myself . . . and think.'

If I believe that one, she'll tell me another. The thought skittered through Zita's mind. But, again, calling Caroline a liar to her face would do no good at all – and would certainly not elicit the real truth.

'And what about Fanny?' Zita asked.

'Fanny?' Caroline said blankly. 'What about her?'

'You *do* remember her, don't you?' Zita heard herself growing caustic. 'Your daughter.'

'I know that.' Caroline gave her an injured look. 'I'm very fond of Fanny. It's just that Jeff suddenly telephoned me and told me that he was sending her over to me for the summer. And it was the worst possible time!'

That bit suddenly had the ring of truth. 'So you dumped her on me.'

'I *trusted* her to you,' Caroline corrected sternly. 'And just look what's happened. I really did think you'd take better care of her.'

There was no doubt about it, Caroline's chief

strength lay in her ability to put the other person in the wrong. Zita began to have a glimmering of the reason – the other reason – why Caroline's husbands were able to face the Divorce Court with such cheerful equanimity.

'I couldn't have been expected to foresee a kidnapping,' Zita said indignantly. 'And if you expected it – I do think you might have warned me. As it is, I still think we should notify the police and let them handle this.

Outside, a sound of rushing water rose above the noise of the storm.

'There's the weir,' Caroline said. 'You'll have to get out on deck and stand by with the mooring rope. The lock's ahead.' There was no mistaking the relief in her voice.

CHAPTER VII

THE LOCK was emptying as they arrived. Zita looped
the mooring rope around one of the posts and, not
bothering to tie it, just held it there while they waited
for their gates to open. Only one other hire craft was
waiting with them. When the gates swung open, they
released a speedboat and two private cruisers into the
downstream current. At this time of day and in this
storm, most of the pleasure boats found it more
pleasurable to tie up for the night and begin cooking
a hot dinner.

Caroline started the boat forward impatiently.
'Stand by,' she ordered, 'to jump ashore when the
water gets high enough. I want you to run down to
the other end of the lock and tell me if you can see
any boats upriver, and what their names are.'

'I do wish – ' Zita began, but Caroline had swung the
boat out without warning and she had to let go of the
rope quickly, before it dislocated her arm, and then
fish it dripping from the water and coil it on the
deck. By that time, they were inside the high wooden
walls of the lock and she had lost her train of
thought. Not that it made any difference. Caroline
did not care what *she* wished.

The swirling waters rapidly lifted the boat, bringing
it to the higher level of the Thames they would soon
sail out into. Caroline watched the lock bank inching

within reach. When it loomed about four feet over the
boat, she shouted, 'Jump!'

'I'm not an acrobat,' Zita said coldly.

'If you don't hurry,' Caroline said, 'you won't have
time to read all the names if there are many boats
there.' It was nothing to her that it was still pouring –
she was sheltered in the wheelhouse.

Zita waited grimly until the bank was a more
reasonable foot and a half above the boat and then
hopped up. She had, she considered, been doing a
little too much jumping lately just because Caroline
had ordered '*Jump!*'

No boats were waiting on the other side for the lock
gates to open. Nor were there any craft in sight.
Obviously, everyone upriver had sensibly moored for
the night. Which meant that all the best mooring
places would be taken and they would be left to try to
tether the boat to some tree branch overhanging a
muddy, slippery bank. If, of course, Caroline didn't
plan to continue sailing all night.

'All right,' Zita said, stepping back into the boat,
which was now level with the top of the lock, 'the
coast is clear.'

Caroline nodded and kicked the motor into action
again, idling it while the lock gates opened slowly.

Zita was glad she had wasted no time getting back
on board – Caroline was showing more signs of im-
patience by the minute, and she had no illusions left.
Caroline would cheerfully abandon anyone who got
in her way or threatened to delay her progress. Not
for the first time, Zita felt a throb of empathy with

Caroline's ex-husbands.

'I'm soaked again,' she commented, not really expecting any response.

Caroline surprised her. 'There's an overnight case at the foot of my bunk. You'll find another sweater in that.'

The case was there, a small black one – like Caroline's current costume, more inconspicuous than one would expect. However, it resisted all efforts to open it.

'The case is locked,' she reported back to Caroline.

Again the boat yawed widely. A faintly flustered expression appeared for the first time on Caroline's face. 'Take the wheel,' she directed. 'Keep us in midstream. I'll see about it.' She disappeared into the cabin, shutting the door behind her.

Keeping the boat on a straight course was, Zita thought, decidedly easier than trying to keep Caroline straight. There was something particularly nasty about the way the boat wavered all over the river when Caroline was faced with an unexpected question. If they could see a chart of their wake along the river, Zita suspected that it would look like the graph of a lie-detector chart – if only one knew how to read it.

'All right.' Caroline came back and repossessed the wheel. 'It's open now. The lock was jammed, that's all.'

What was Caroline trying to pull? The case that was lying open on the bunk was not the case that had been locked. It was very similar, but this one had a thin red band running along the rim, the metal lock and hinges bore a closer resemblance to silver, it was slimmer and lighter in weight. In all, a sleeker case, and the sort one would more easily associate with Caroline. There was no trace of the other case to be seen.

As promised, a black sweater lay on top of the clothes inside. Zita picked it up. More dark folds of wool lay beneath it. How many black sweaters had Caroline packed – and why? Because black was an inconspicuous colour? Because it could not be easily seen at night?

Zita picked up the second sweater and shook it out – it was a child's size. She dropped it on the bunk while she pulled off her wet sweater and put the dry one on. Then she returned to the wheelhouse, carrying the child's sweater. 'What *has* happened to Fanny?' she asked.

Automatically, she braced herself as the boat veered sharply and Caroline spun the wheel about to bring it back on course.

'I wish you'd stop saying things like that,' Caroline complained. 'I keep telling you – nothing's happened to Fanny. She's perfectly all right. We're going to get her now.'

'Where is she?'

'Upriver – ' Caroline gestured vaguely. 'Just a bit farther. We're nearly there.'

'Where?'

Caroline didn't answer.

'Put me ashore,' Zita said grimly. 'I've had quite enough. I'm going to the police.'

Caroline twitched and the boat nearly ran aground. 'Don't be so silly,' she said.

'Silly?' Zita snapped. 'A nine-year-old child is kidnapped from my house and you tell me not to be silly. I don't believe you know where she is. She could be anywhere – frightened . . . alone . . . hurt . . .'

'That's nonsense,' Caroline said. 'She'd never be harmed. Xavier adores children.'

'Xavier!' At last, Caroline had let something slip. 'What has *he* to do with Fanny? Isn't he on his yacht in the Med – ?' She broke off, realizing that she had long ago ceased to believe in that mythological yachting trip.

'It's a personal matter,' Caroline said. 'You . . . you may have gathered that we . . . aren't the friends we used to be. I was afraid he might do something completely stupid, like this. That's why I sent Fanny to you. I thought she'd be safe there.'

'Do you mean that Xavier has kidnapped Fanny in order to get some sort of revenge on you?'

'Now you're being melodramatic.' But the boat had given a guilty swerve again. 'He just thinks . . . oh, I don't know. I suppose he thinks he'll have some sort of hold over me if he's got Fanny. I told you – it's a personal matter. But, of course,' she added airily, 'he mustn't be allowed to get away with it.'

'*Why* should Xavier want a hold over you?' Like most of Caroline's explanations, this one explained the barest minimum – and barely held water.

'We're there!' There was a trace of relief in Caroline's voice. The boat veered towards a small dock belonging to one of the riverside houses. 'Let's get Fanny first – we can talk later. What time is it?'

'Quarter to ten.'

'Then that's all right. They'll have put her to bed ages ago.' Caroline cut off the motor and the boat moved silently towards the shore. 'We can slip up the back stairs and get her.'

'How are we going to get in?' A house was just visible as a dark outline through the storm. It appeared to be an eighteenth-century folly which had been renovated as a weekend cottage. Or, possibly, a Victorian idea of a suitable holiday home. No glimmer of light brightened the dark hulk at any point. It looked brooding and forbidding – a house which had battened down the hatches against both storm and intruders.

'Oh . . . well . . . uh . . . probably we'll find a door open,' Caroline said evasively. 'They don't always lock up as well as they should.'

'I see,' Zita said, interpreting this as meaning that Caroline had her own key, but did not want to admit it. 'And suppose we get caught?'

'I don't see why you always have to look on the dark side of everything!' Caroline snapped. 'We won't even be seen. There's a back staircase. The only room suitable for Fanny would be the one at the head of that staircase. It used to be the maid's room. We can be in and out – with Fanny – and no one will ever know until tomorrow morning when they go to bring her breakfast.'

It sounded workable, bearing in mind that Caroline undoubtedly knew a lot more about the layout of the house and the routine of its inhabitants than she was openly admitting.

The boat nudged the little pier. A large iron mooring ring glistered wetly against the dull wet shine of the wooden dock. Automatically, Zita picked up the mooring rope and made the boat fast. There were too many questions in her mind, but she knew that Caroline would refuse to answer any of them – or else sidestep so nimbly that asking them would be a waste of time.

And, with Fanny so close, they could not waste time now. First, they must get Fanny safe aboard the cabin cruiser – remove the pawn from whatever complicated game Caroline and Xavier were playing with each other. Then, perhaps, Caroline might be induced to answer some questions.

The long twisting, slightly uphill path to the house was muddy and slippery. Naturally, Caroline led the way. Equally naturally, it never occurred to her to flash the light from the tiny pencil torch behind her occasionally to help Zita.

Grinding her teeth, Zita tried to pick her way along, tripping and slipping. If they got out of this, she vowed grimly, she would have learned her lesson. She would never associate with Caroline again. The Iron Curtain would come down on Caroline's Friend of the Family act. And, if David objected – well, he could just choose between them.

'Here.' Caroline stopped so abruptly that Zita bumped into her. They were both shapeless black blobs in the rainy darkness. Above them loomed a larger, blacker mass.

'Wait here,' Caroline directed, 'while I try the door. It's probably open.'

Zita didn't say anything. She heard the scratching of a key being fumbled into a lock, and the rasp of the lock turning. She was thankful that the darkness made it unnecessary to arrange her face into a suitably gullible expression. Acting was best left to actors — and to extremely talented amateurs, like Caroline.

'It *is* open,' Caroline said blandly. 'I *thought* it would be.'

'How very fortunate,' Zita murmured, but irony was lost on Caroline.

'Isn't it?' she agreed. 'Mind the step. The back stairs are to the left. Be careful. I don't think we dare risk a light, although everybody is probably at the front of the house watching television.'

The darkness was of a paler grey quality inside the door. Somewhere at the front of the house, there was a light. Despite this, the house had an unoccupied feeling about it.

The stairs were narrow, steep and winding. They *would* be, Zita thought bitterly. Caroline moved up them smoothly and noiselessly. Zita was uncomfortably aware of the shuffling noise she made as her foot groped for each step.

It didn't help when Caroline turned abruptly and said, 'Shhh!'

Zita bit down on an answer which would have been rude, belligerent and far too high-pitched. As soon as

they were safely out of this, she would allow herself
the luxury of telling Caroline exactly what she
thought of her and then severing all diplomatic relations for ever. She clung to the shining promise of
that thought as to a rock.

Caroline reached the top of the stairs and, no longer
needing it herself, thoughtfully flashed the torch on
the few steps remaining for Zita to climb.

'Thank you,' Zita said coldly.

'Not so loud!' Caroline snapped. 'We don't want to
frighten Fanny. If she makes a disturbance, they'll
come up here and find us.'

Zita heard the click of the latch as the doorknob
turned. A widening sliver of grey appeared in the
darkness in front of them.

'Fanny? Don't be frightened, darling – it's Mummy,'
Caroline cooed softly. 'Fanny, it's Mummy. Don't say
anything. Just be quiet and we'll run away from here
and hide. Won't that be a lovely new game? Fanny
. . . Fanny – ?'

The splinter of light from Caroline's torch stabbed
wildly around the room.

'Fanny – ?' The light hesitated on the rumpled bed.
Someone had obviously been sleeping there earlier,
but it was empty now.

'Fanny – ?' A pillow lay near the bed, as though it
had been hurled out. Or as though someone had been
clinging to it when lifted up.

'She isn't here!' Caroline's whisper rose shrilly.
'She's gone!'

'Shhh!' Zita cautiously crossed the room to a dim

square of grey on the other side. She groped for the shade and pulled it down. 'Put the light on,' she said. 'We'll have to risk it.'

Caroline shut the door and the click of a switch flooded the room with a brightness that left them blinking.

'Fanny – ?' Caroline stooped to look under the bed.

'Fanny – ?' Zita opened the closet door.

That took care of any possible hiding-places. They looked at each other.

'Perhaps she's downstairs.' Caroline's tone denied any belief in the possibility. 'Perhaps they've let her stay up late to watch television.'

'Perhaps.' The mute evidence of the pillow seemed to tell a different story. Zita picked it up, turning it over thoughtfully before replacing it on the bed. Not even to herself was she willing to admit that she was checking it for traces of blood or saliva.

Fanny, despite her mental toughness, was too small and frail to put up much of a fight. It would have taken very little effort. But, surely, no one would smother a child –

'She must be downstairs,' Caroline said. 'She *must* be.'

'There's no way we can be sure she was ever here at all,' Zita tried to think sanely. Caroline looked ready to slip over the edge of hysteria.

'Where else could she have been?' Her voice went higher and Caroline took a deep breath, obviously recognizing the danger herself. 'This was the only place they could have taken her. If she isn't here . . .

then . . . then . . . I don't know *where* she is!'

'We'd better look downstairs,' Zita said. 'Are you up to it? I can find the way, if – '

'I'm all right,' Caroline said. 'You'd just get lost.' She led the way from the room, leaving the door open and the light on, marching resolutely down the stairs, no longer trying to be quiet.

Zita snapped off the light and followed uneasily. Caroline may have nerved herself for a showdown, but she wasn't sure she was prepared for one herself. Xavier had no idea who she was, and she did not like the thought of being witness to some personal quarrel which seemed about to flare up into a bitter scene.

Pausing at the kitchen door, Caroline flipped a switch. Fluorescent lights flickered on overhead. Caroline stalked through the compact, ultra-modern kitchen, her footsteps resounding challengingly. Only the hum of the refrigerator sounded in answer.

Again, Caroline stabbed at a light switch, not to turn off the kitchen lights, but to illuminate the hallway. The walls were dark red, the carpet the colour of dried blood. Ahead of them, the door was ajar and the lights were already lit in the room behind the door.

Caroline slowed as they approached the door, but her tread was still resolute. 'Xavier,' she called, 'it's me. I've come to get my child!' She took another deep breath and flung the door open.

It was a red, red room. Brooding and sinister. The walls and carpet were an extension of the colour scheme in the hall. The sofa and chairs were upholstered in dark maroon leather. An obsidian marble

coffee-table glittered on iron legs. The walls were hung
with paintings of blood and flame and shadows: cities
of smoking ruins; figures encased in layered armadillo-
like armour – or scales. The objets d'art scattered
around the room were also the new sort, 'anthropo-
morphic tool boxes' David called them: nuts, bolts,
flywheels, spanners, welded into shapes resembling
human beings and bronzed. Spanner Crusaders, with
bolted heads, warred with each other over supine
chainsaw-and-nut maidens, while cogwheel and gear-
box horses reared in the background.

What would you say of a man who could live in
such a room? How would you read his character?
It was suddenly, vitally important to Zita that she
should be able to interpret Xavier.

A madman? Or a romantic? Or both – one side of
his nature fighting the other? Certainly, he must be
brooding, merciless – and cruel?

Zita looked at the paintings again, trying to take
refuge in abstract thoughts. Trying not to look at the
man lying beside the obsidian table, the rivulets of
blood from his wounds drying to the same colour as
the carpet they were soaking into.

Caroline stood frozen beside her. Someone had to
move, they could not stay there indefinitely. With a
sigh she barely recognized as her own, Zita moved into
the room.

Knowing it was useless, she knelt and reached for
his pulse. He had been lying on his side and, as she
moved the cooling, clammy hand, the body stirred,
rolled on to its back.

Zita let go and stepped back. It was the short stocky man who had been watching the house. The one she had thought to be an American – had believed to be Fanny's father.

Caroline screamed. 'Oh, God – it's Melancholy!' She crumpled into a sobbing little heap on the floor.

CHAPTER VIII

HYSTERIA WAS all they needed at this moment! Zita crossed the room swiftly, yanked Caroline to her feet and shook her. Then reflected regretfully that she had probably just lost her last chance of legitimately slapping Caroline's face, for Caroline was already getting herself under control.

'Who is he?' They both avoided looking at the body beside the obsidian table. 'Do you know him?'

'He's Melancholy.' Caroline drew a deep shuddering breath. 'Everyone called him that. His real name was Melankopolous – or something like that. He's Xavier's right-hand man . . . He *was*.'

'It can't have happened too long ago,' Zita said. 'He – he was still warm.'

Caroline shuddered again, but in a curiously withdrawn sort of way. She looked as though she were listening to private voices who were, perhaps, explaining something to her. Either that, or she was plotting something else. Her gaze began to rove about the room searchingly.

'Where's the telephone?' Zita asked. She had not seen one in any of the rooms they had been in so far.

'Telephone?' Caroline was curiously vague. 'What do you want a telephone for?'

'To call the police,' Zita said. 'This changes everything. We'll *have* to report this – and the kidnapping,

too.' Even Caroline must understand that the whole
thing could no longer be regarded as an unfortunate
aftermath of a lover's quarrel. The situation was out of
control and there was no way she could retrieve it.
A man was dead – no amount of winsome apology
was going to undo that.

'Fanny – ' Caroline said, still vague, but with the
beginnings of alarm. 'Where is she? Perhaps – ' she
grasped hopefully at the straw she had discarded upstairs – 'perhaps she never *was* here.'

Zita had been looking around the room herself. There
was one note out of key: a touch of fawn suede protruding at the back of the sofa, spoiling the mordant
symphony of reds and blacks. She crossed the room
and stood, looking down.

'Romeo!' She bent and picked up the toy.

'What?' Caroline was startled at the exclamation,
more startled as she saw the spotted suede giraffe with
the ridiculous long eyelashes.

'It's Fanny's,' Zita told her. 'She bought it after you
left us at the airport. She had it with her when she was
taken from my house.'

'Then she was here,' Caroline said dully.

'*And* she was in this room.' Zita forced the knowledge on her. 'Fanny always took the doll to bed with
her. She must have been awakened – perhaps by quar-
relling – and come downstairs, still clutching Romeo.
She dropped him when she saw what was happening –
or when they discovered her.'

'You don't know that,' Caroline said. 'Perhaps she
was asleep, and they carried her through the room,

and someone dropped the toy and didn't stop for it.'

'We can't be sure,' Zita agreed. 'But the chances are that Fanny knows what happened here. For heaven's sake!' Her frayed temper abruptly snapped at Caroline's continued wilful obtuseness.

'Don't you see? This makes her a witness. A nine-year-old child is old enough to testify – in Judge's Chambers, if not in open Court. She's dangerous to them now. We've got to get all the help we can to get her back safely. We *must* call in the police.'

'We can't,' Caroline said.

'Why on earth not?'

Caroline glanced around and shuddered. 'We can't talk here,' she said. 'Turn the lights off and let's get back to the boat and I – I'll tell you why not.'

The rain hadn't slackened. Grimly intent, Zita followed Caroline back to the boat. They could do nothing at the house. Boarding the boat, Caroline spoke for the first time.

'I wonder what's happened to Cheerful,' she said.

'Cheerful?'

'He was always with Melancholy. They were a sort of team. They ran Xavier's affairs – those he didn't take care of personally. *His* real name was Chiropodist – or something like that, so everyone called him – '

'Cheerful,' Zita finished, thinking hysterically that Xavier and his crew were beginning to sound like Snow White and the Seven Dwarfs. Only, who was the Wicked Stepmother?

'There, that's better.' Caroline snapped on the cabin

light and smiled at Zita with a melting innocence.
'We'll put the kettle on, have a cup of tea, and dry
out – '

'Let's just have a few facts.' Zita propped Romeo
against the foot of her bunk. 'I'm still waiting to hear
why you don't want the police brought into this.'

'Because it isn't necessary. I've told you – it's a
personal matter between Xavier and me. We can
settle it ourselves. We don't want any nasty publicity.'

Could Caroline really be so adept at self-deception
as she seemed to be? Snow-White-Caroline, who undoubtedly thought of Xavier as Grumpy and believed
she had only to tweak his hair and pout prettily at
him in order to resolve all their little differences. And
then Grumpy-Xavier would blush and bridle and hand
back Little Fanny, and all would be peaches and cream
again.

Except that the Wicked Stepmother had stabbed
fat friendly Melancholy and left him to die in the
Enchanted Cottage – and nothing was ever going to
be so simple again. The path to the Happy Ending had
ended in a steep sharp drop into a pit.

'There'll be publicity when that body is found.' Zita
tried to call Caroline to order.

'Oh yes,' Caroline said vaguely. 'But perhaps it won't
be found. At least, not there. And no one will ever
know *we* were there, if we keep quiet. So, all we have
to do is keep quiet, and everything will be all right.
You see,' she finished triumphantly, 'nothing has
changed, after all.'

'You mean someone else will move the body. Perhaps

dispose of it altogether.' Of course, the Good Fairies would not desert dear Snow White. Someone had left a bowl of bread and milk under the table and the Brownies would come in the night and tidy up all the nasty mess.

'Doesn't it bother you at all – ' Zita spoke slowly and distinctly, as though to someone not quite bright – 'that your daughter is in the hands of a murderer?'

'Oh, Xavier didn't do it.' Caroline had absolute faith. 'He'd never have hurt Melancholy. And he won't harm Fanny, either. I keep telling you that.'

Zita ignored the vote of confidence. 'If he didn't do it, then who did?'

'*I* don't know.' Caroline looked vaguely disturbed. 'Of course, a man in Xavier's position always has lots of enemies.' She brightened. 'But he has lots of friends, too.'

Who, presumably, would do the necessary tidying up. Zita sighed deeply. 'I suppose there's no use in appealing to your sense of civic duty?'

'You *are* dreary,' Caroline pouted. 'You go on and on about things – just like David. You're very well-matched, you know. I used to think you were too good for him, but I was wrong. You're just as dreary and petty-minded as he is.'

That was too much! She was not going to stand here and let Caroline dissect her marriage – or her husband.

'What does Xavier want?' Zita asked bluntly.

'I told you – ' Caroline's eyelashes fluttered down.

'I don't care *how* personal it is. You've pulled me into the middle of this mess and I have a right to know. Otherwise, I *will* call the police!'

'Oh, all right,' Caroline sulked. 'What do you think he wants? He wants money.'

'Xavier?' Zita asked incredulously. Somehow, it was the last thing she had expected. *'He* wants money from *you?* You can't mean he's going bankrupt? With all the money he's been making from those gambling clubs of his – '

'Oh, well,' Caroline said, 'that's the money he wants.'

'What?'

'I was entitled to it – ' Caroline was instantly defensive. 'After all the time I threw away on him! And I let that nice Brazilian millionaire go by. Because I thought Xavier and I – And then I found out that sneak was married. He'd been married all the time! To some dreary little creature he hides away in Greece. And he said he had no intention of divorcing her. He owed me something for that – and I took it.'

'You took it,' Zita said weakly. Even for Caroline, this was beyond the pale.

'Naturally,' Caroline said. 'I'd earned it.'

'But Xavier doesn't think so.'

'Oh, *him!* He'll cool down and be reasonable, just as soon as he's had time to think things over. He can't go to the police because he'd have to explain what he was doing with that much money in his wall safe. And that would mean admitting that he was fiddling his income tax returns.'

'And *you* can't go to the police,' Zita said slowly, 'because you'd have to admit that you'd stolen his money.'

'Finally, you're getting the point,' Caroline said crossly. 'But I told you, I *earned* that money.'

'Except that the police might not see it that way. And, obviously, Xavier doesn't.'

'Well, he wouldn't, would he?' Caroline looked thoughtful. 'I wonder how he found out already? I mean, I didn't take it all. I left so much he might never have noticed. He must count it every night.' She seemed struck by a new idea. 'Do you think he's a secret miser – or heading that way?'

'I think – ' Zita could not continue. Any declaration of what she really thought would only cloud the issue. The one important thing at the moment was to rescue Fanny – while there was still time.

'I suppose we'd better cast off,' Caroline said, as though following her train of thought in a dim way. 'There's nothing more we can do here.'

Silently, Zita stepped ashore and loosed the mooring rope. Caroline's gift for understatement was not, it appeared, going to desert her now. However, it was true that there was nothing more they *could* do here – although there were several things they *ought* to do. But Caroline had won. There was no question now of calling in the police. The only question was whether Xavier were really as child-loving as Caroline claimed – and whether they would get Fanny back safely . . .

The rain had stopped and, although the moon had not been so reckless as to actually come out, a faint

veining of light glimmered through clouds. The cabin
cruiser glided downriver, so quietly that they could
hear the soft swish of their wash curling against the
shore.

'It's quarter past eleven,' Caroline calculated. 'We
won't be able to get through any more locks tonight.
That is,' she qualified, 'we probably could, but – '

'But we don't want to draw attention to ourselves.'
Zita overlooked Caroline's serene assurance that all
locks would be opened to them if she chose to exert
her charm. She was conscious of a vague surprise that
it was only quarter past eleven – she seemed to have
been trapped in this day for ever, like an insect in
amber, never to get free.

'We can tie up outside the lock,' Caroline went on,
as though she had not spoken. 'And I'll take the boat
through first thing in the morning.'

There was something odd about that statement. Zita
tried to focus her mind on the words, in order to
dissect and analyse them.

'The railway station is just a ten-minute walk along
the towpath from the lock,' Caroline continued.
'There's a midnight train you can take back to town.'

'Back to town?' Zita echoed blankly. She had, she
realized, been thinking longingly of the bunk in the
cabin – it now began to shimmer like the mirage of an
oasis before a parched desert traveller.

'Well, you don't expect *me* to go, do you?' Caroline
snapped. 'I've got to stay with the boat. That means
you'll have to go to my flat – to see if there's any post.
If they've been trying to contact me, we want to know

as soon as possible.'

'I could handle the boat,' Zita suggested weakly, feeling overwhelmed by the force of Caroline's personality. How could Caroline have gone through so much in the past forty-eight hours or so and remained so untouched by it? Did anything really reach her, or was she so absorbed in her own fantasies that the real world rolled past unnoticed?

Zita leaned against the cabin door jamb. She was exhausted, weakening rapidly with hunger, damply uncomfortable, and overwhelmed by the feeling that she could no longer cope with the situation. Also, she missed David desperately.

David! – the thought turned from wistful to venomous. This was all his fault! He was responsible for her being here at this moment, listening to this madwoman. *Other* men had nice uncivilized divorces and never spoke to their ex-wives again. In fact, *other* men exercised considerably more care in the choice of woman they married –

She let that train of thought die away, recognizing that a flaw had crept into the reasoning. However, the jolt of adrenalin from the brief fury had done her a world of good. She felt almost able to manage again.

'. . . change back into your suit?' Caroline had never stopped talking, planning. 'You can wear the jeans, if you like, but I'm afraid it might make you rather conspicuous – and we want to avoid that, don't we?'

Perhaps Caroline was, for once, able to interpret correctly the sudden dangerous flash in another woman's eyes. Her own violet eyes went wider and very earnest.

'It really *is* good of you,' she added hastily. 'I *do* appreciate it. It's just – ' she blinked unconvincingly – there was no trace of tears in those wide scheming eyes – 'it's just that I'm so worried about little Fanny. Oh, I *know* she's perfectly all right with Xavier. It's just that – '

The memory of the cooling body oozing blood into the deep red carpet beside the obsidian table rose between them. Caroline made a denying, dismissive gesture with one hand, her eyes genuinely clouded for a moment.

'It's just that one can't foresee everything,' Zita said, finishing the sentence for her.

'Precisely!' Caroline grasped the straw gratefully, before observing that it was broken and splintered. She gave Zita a wounded look.

'I was going to suggest,' she said righteously, ignoring the pitfalls all around, 'that you stay the night at my flat. It won't be easy to get transport at that hour.' A fairly mild understatement.

'Even taxis – ' a delicate shading in her undertone hinted *if you could possibly afford one for that distance* – 'will be unobtainable. 'No – ' her voice firmed and strengthened – 'you'd best stay the night. In the morning, you can go back to your own place, and I'll come straight there later in the day. That's probably where Xavier will try to contact me, anyway. But you must go to the flat first – just in case he's sent a message there.'

It was a perfectly reasonable, sensible plan. Only her growing antipathy towards Caroline made her hesitate. Zita realized this and kept her peace as Caroline rummaged in a handbag and brought out a key, rather ostentatiously, in hallmarked gold. (The sort of thing sometimes given as a coming-of-age birthday present – but Caroline was a long way from eighteen. It was useless, however, trying to determine just what Caroline was ever trying to prove.)

'Here.' Caroline tossed it to her. 'Now, hadn't you better change? We'll be there soon.'

Downriver, a distant glow against the stormy sky hinted at a town in the offing. Caroline veered the boat towards it purposefully.

Zita hovered in the cabinway a moment, but Caroline ignored her. There was obviously nothing more she felt like saying. Because there was nothing more to say? Or because any further conversation might reveal more of matters Caroline had so coyly – and perhaps inaccurately – referred to as 'personal'?

Surrendering, Zita went into the cabin. Her skirt was still damp at the hem, but a certain amount of the mud brushed off. She kept the black sweater and, over it, the jacket was not unbearably uncomfortable.

She was attempting to put her face into good enough order to show in public when the boat thudded into a mooring dock with a bump that sent her lipstick sliding up and across her cheek like a razor slash.

A most uncomfortable thought. Zita wiped the lipstick streak off carefully and tried again with the lipstick, achieving better results. Outside, she could hear

Caroline coping quite adequately with the mooring procedure. Caroline could always cope by herself – when she had to.

Zita looked around the cabin carefully, as Caroline began calling to her impatiently. Nothing of hers seemed to be left behind; but then, she hadn't brought much with her. Not unnaturally – who could have imagined a day ending like this?

Just before she left, on a sudden impulse, she took Romeo from the bunk. Caroline would never remember him – Caroline always had more important affairs to worry about – and Fanny would be *so* glad to see her doll again. If, indeed, any of *them* ever saw Fanny again. But that didn't bear thinking about. Fanny *must* be safe, *must* come back to them unharmed.

Clutching Romeo to her – for all the world like Fanny herself seeking comfort from him – Zita picked up her handbag and went out on to the deck.

CHAPTER IX

THE SMOOTH gold key glided effortlessly into the gilded lock and turned without struggle. A faint, exotic perfume wafted to her nostrils as Zita stepped into the hallway. A moment's groping found a wall switch, and a discreet rose-shaded light suffused the hallway. She moved forward cautiously, but intrigued. She had never been in Caroline's flat before.

Mmmm, it was lovely. Every magazine illustration you had ever seen of the Home Beautiful – and a few you had never been able to imagine. Frighteningly modern, desperately chic, completely ultra-ultra, and expensive. Very expensive. Only a cat would wonder who paid for it all.

Xavier, Zita assumed. No wonder Caroline had been so upset to discover that he preferred a more primitive bliss in his own country, with his own kind, and that her lease on all this luxury was a tenuous one, and not the freehold she had expected. Yes, it was enough to make any lady go on the turn – let alone Caroline.

The lounge, as one might have expected had one thought about it, was sunken. Not having thought about it, Zita stumbled down into it. Her flailing arms struck a concealed switch and suitably concealed lighting sprang into life.

At first glance, multi-coloured cushions seemed to be floating in mid-air above a foamy white carpet.

Another glance revealed the clear plastic inflated chairs and sofa they were actually resting on.

Deep red glass ashtrays and a cigarette box could not possibly be suspended above a frame of spidery iron legs, and a closer look brought the sheet glass tabletop into focus. Brought too the thought that she had seen that shade of red before. Xavier's trademark – she shuddered.

It was an uneasy room, for all its expensive chic. Insubstantial, unanchored – rather like Caroline herself.

Zita propped Romeo against the fragile white-painted table leg, and sat down, groping in her bag for her cigarettes. (She could *not* touch that dark red cigarette box. She felt uncomfortable even dropping the used match into the spotless dark red ashtray.)

She felt even more uneasy about leaning back in the plastic chair. Although it was perfectly comfortable, it seemed somehow transient. Hostage to every carelessly flicked cigarette ash or sharp heel. She now noticed, too, a thin hairline crack across a corner of the glass tabletop. No, Caroline's furniture would never make old bones.

At the rate she was going, neither would Caroline.

Zita stood up abruptly and stubbed out her cigarette. She had come here to look for a message from Xavier and she had better get on with it.

Half-a-dozen unopened letters were propped up on small glass shelves suspended against the farther wall by thin wires dropping from the ceiling moulding. The shelving swayed perilously as she lifted the letters

from it. Most of them were postmarked at least a fortnight ago. How long had Caroline been in hiding?

In the hallway, a sort of rigid cobweb held several
more letters suspended between the mail slot and the
floor. None had been posted since Fanny's disappear-
ance. One, indeed, was addressed to Fanny c/o Caroline – a postcard of the Taj Mahal and a jocular message signed Daddy.

Knowing Fanny, Zita could not imagine her amused
by the message. But perhaps Fanny had a different
personality in the bosom of her family – many people
had. On impulse, she thrust the card into her handbag.
To give to Fanny when . . . when she saw her again.
She felt, somehow, as though it were a talisman to
prove that she *would* see Fanny again.

At the bottom of the cobweb lurked a folded sheet
of lined paper. Zita pulled it out hurriedly, scarcely
noticing the fingernail she splintered against the hard
fibre of the cobweb as she did so.

Uneven words, written in green Biro, straggled
across the pale blue lines:

Dear Madam,

This is the third time as I have come here and no
sign of you, and no money neither. Perhaps you
would be good enough to let me know if you still
require my services, and when.

Yours faithfully,
Mrs (blot).

Zita refolded the sheet of paper and slipped it back
into the cobweb. Mrs Blot had put her finger on the
crux of the matter. *When?*

When would they hear? When would they have Fanny safely back again. When?

She replaced the rest of the mail, not able to dream that Caroline might be interested in anything else in the world while Fanny was still in jeopardy. Certainly not in the oversized envelope, addressed in a florid hand, and bearing Brazilian air mail stamps.

There were no other messages in the front hall. But it was a fallacy, of course, to assume that Xavier must confine himself to the formality of the post. Presumably, he had the run of the flat. Probably with his own gold key to match Caroline's.

At the end of the hallway, a small but very modern kitchen was in keeping with the rest of the flat. There was a curious emptiness to it. The cupboard shelves were not so well stocked as those in the galley of the cabin cruiser. The infra-red oven did not look as though it had ever been used for anything more challenging than heating up a frozen TV-dinner.

A narrow, mirrored passageway ran from the kitchen past the half-opened door of a bathroom. (She didn't investigate – that bath was probably sunken, too.) It ended at a closed door which must open into the bedroom. Arguing silently to herself that Caroline had forfeited any right to privacy, Zita opened the door and stepped inside, reaching for the light switch.

Indirect lighting subtly illuminated the room, leaving strategically shadowed areas. A darkened glade by the french window which opened, as Zita remembered from her survey of the façade of the block, on to a vine-covered balcony. Another swirl of shadows in a corner by a lattice-work folding screen hinted at a discreetly indiscreet disrobing.

As might have been expected, the largest, most romantically shadowed area was the pool of darkness surrounding the large double bed. (Someone had gone to a great deal of trouble equipping this room with what was practically stage lighting – only a few spotlights were missing.)

A froth of white veiling cascaded from a high coronet, in Empire style. The gleam of a satin bedspread shimmered faintly out of the darkness, again in an improbably virginal white.

It was only on a closer look that one could discern a form lying on the bed.

'Oh, I'm sorry,' Zita gasped. 'I'm terribly sorry. I had no idea anyone was here.' She backed towards the door, but there was no sound or movement from the bed. She might not have spoken at all. In fact, it was too quiet.

She hesitated, then advanced slowly and softly. But she need not have worried about disturbing him.

There was no expression in the blank eyes which did not quite focus upon her approach. The shirt, she saw, drawing closer, was not spotted as she had supposed, but streaked with dried blood. The heavy form seemed thicker than ever, perhaps because it had stiffened imperceptibly. She had seen him before – more recently dead. He did not improve upon second sight. He was Melancholy – what was left of Melancholy.

She had found a message from Xavier, after all . . .

She backed out of the extravagant bedroom on tiptoe, closing the door silently behind her, recognizing as she did so the futility of trying not to disturb someone who could never be disturbed again.

She ought to call the police. But that was more impossible than ever now. A corpse in Caroline's bed would be even more difficult and embarrassing to explain than a corpse in Xavier's cottage – and would engender even more uninhibited newspaper headlines. The moment had long since passed when the police could still have been called.

Was that what Xavier had intended? Or did he not know that they had discovered the body the first time, in the cottage? Had he brought it here to be found by Caroline upon her return, thinking that she would then be forced to call upon him to dispose of the body, save her from a potential notoriety worse than anything she had yet experienced?

But Caroline had no intention of returning – at least, not for some time yet. Not until the whole situation had been sorted out and Fanny recovered. By then, Xavier might have moved his dead henchman, either to some final resting-place, or to some less ambiguous place to be discovered.

Besides, as Caroline herself would have pointed out, you can't be blamed for ignoring or going contrary to instructions if the message never reached you. It was unlikely that Xavier knew they had been in the cottage. (They must have arrived during the interval when he was absent, moving Fanny to a different hiding-place before coming back to move Melancholy.) If there was, likewise, no evidence of anyone's presence in the flat, he would never be sure that Caroline had received his grim message.

Snapping the lights off along the way, she returned to the lounge. There was very little trace of her passage in the room. Reluctantly, she replaced Fanny's postcard from her father on the glass shelves – in case Xavier had noticed it there. Nothing else being available, she emptied the ashtray into her handbag – she could clean it out later – and polished the ashtray to remove finger-marks. She was polishing the glass shelves and trying to remember which doorknobs she had touched when common sense reasserted itself. Xavier wasn't going to go through the flat with a fiingerprinting kit. He'd just take a quick look around to see if anything had been disturbed.

Once he had seen that having left the body here had had no effect, Xavier would undoubtedly move it again. Only the police would worry about fingerprints – and it wouldn't come to that. If it did, well, she had a right to be in Caroline's flat. She was at least an acquaintance, if not a friend. Although Caroline, in her own quaint reckoning, seemed to feel that a common husband made them some sort of sisters-in-law.

She tucked Romeo firmly under her arm and took a final look around the room. It looked the way it had when she arrived. Possibly an expert might be able to tell someone had moved through it, but she doubted that that was the sort of thing Xavier was expert at.

Reluctantly, she dismissed the idea of telephoning for a minicab from this line. (Phone tapping was probably one of the things he *was* good at.) It was a long

way home to Islington and the chances of picking up
a taxi at this hour of the night – or, rather, this hour
of the morning – were slim. But a long walk would do
her good and might even help to clarify some of her
thoughts.

At that, the journey wasn't too bad. She managed to
catch one of the strange night service buses, which
glide like phantom coaches through the darkest, lone-
liest hours. Once aboard, Romeo had occasioned much
amusement. (And Caroline had made her change out
of those dry, comfortable jeans in order not to attract
any attention!)

At her own front door, putting her key into the
lock, panic suddenly siezed her. She had a wild, hysterical notion that she would find Melancholy inside.
On *her* bed, perhaps, or propped up on the Victorian
sofa. She had the conviction that he had become her
own personal albatross, and she was doomed to be
haunted by him for the rest of her life.

It was silly – the house was empty, of course. She
went through it, to be sure. She was in the studio when
the telephone rang downstairs. Xavier had lost no time
in making contact.

She wondered, rushing downstairs, whether he had
tried to call earlier and, if so, what his mood would
be. Annoyed? Suspicious? Would he take it out on
Fanny in some way? She snatched up the phone.

'Hello – ?' Her throat was nearly too dry to speak.
'Hello? Hello?' Her frayed temper snapped abruptly.
'For God's sake, don't play games! I know you're there.

Say what you've got to say – and let us know the worst!'

'Zita, is that you?' The warm familiar voice stunned her momentarily. 'What the hell is going on there?'

'David? David – where *are* you?'

'In New York, of course. What – ?'

'But . . . there was no operator.'

'There's direct dialling now. It's a great innovation. Provided, of course, the other party is at home. Where the hell have you been?'

'Been?' There was too much to tell, too much to go into. He could be of no help from three thousand miles away.

'Yes, *been.*' There was no mistaking it. He was furious. Furious – and suspicious. 'What time is it?'

'Time?' She calculated swiftly. 'Why, it's . . . it's ten o'clock.'

'It's ten o'clock *here*, you mean. It's three bloody a.m. *there*. I've been ringing at half-hour intervals since four o'clock this afternoon. Four o'clock *here* – nine o'clock *there*. I asked you a question – where the hell have you been?'

'I've been out,' Zita said faintly.

'Obviously.' Sarcasm coloured the voice. He sounded as though he were just across the street. Zita was suddenly glad that he wasn't. This David was a stranger to her. 'Even my menial intelligence was able to work that out. Perhaps I should rephrase the question: *Where* were you "out" – and with *whom*?'

'Just out,' Zita said, still more faintly. 'With Caroline.'

'Caroline?'

'You remember Caroline.' Zita's voice grew stronger, a trace of asperity sharpening it. 'Your last wife.'

'You mean –' he tried to clarify it – 'Caroline was out – until *this* hour – with *you*?'

Put that way, it sounded a lot more unlikely.

'Yes,' Zita said, feeling that the conversation was getting away from her.

'Caroline,' David said flatly, 'is on a yacht in the Mediterranean. That's why you got landed with Fanny.'

'*I'm* not a liar,' Zita refuted indignantly. 'Caroline *didn't* go on that yachting cruise. She never intended to – if there *was* a cruise to begin with. And Fanny –' She broke off. Even from three thousand miles away, there *was* one thing David could do. He could ring Scotland Yard and bring the police into this. The one thing to be avoided at all costs. For once, she was in agreement with Caroline about something.

'I see,' David said, in the maddening tones of someone trying to humour an imbecile. 'You and Caroline had a nice cozy evening together. All alone? Or did you keep the child up till this hour, too?'

'Of course not,' Zita said. 'That is . . . I mean –' Again she broke off. If Fanny had been there, then the telephone would have awakened her. She would have answered it. She was such a nosy-parkering little brat, she'd have *had* to answer it. And David, having had some experience of Fanny, knew it.

'Yes?' His voice was cold and remote. '*Tell* me what you mean.'

Zita damned Caroline silently. Damned her to hell and perdition. For getting her into this, for being such a miserable wife, in the first place, that she had destroyed so much of David's self-confidence. Left him uncertain and suspicious, unable to trust again. Ready to believe the worst of any woman – especially his wife.

'And while you're at it,' the icy voice continued, 'tell me who else you had along on your cozy little double date.'

It was a nightmare. Nightmare on top of nightmare. Their first major quarrel, three thousand miles apart, unable to see each other, reduced to two angry voices snarling at each other across an ocean.

'David, please –' To her annoyance, she heard her voice shaking. She knew it was the final reaction to the long nerve-racking day. But to David, would it sound like guilt?

'David, I promise you – it wasn't like that at all. I can explain, but – '

'Go ahead,' he said. 'I'm waiting. I've been waiting for hours.'

'But not now.' She regained control of her voice. 'Not . . . like this.'

'You refuse, then,' he said coldly.

'It's not that I refuse – it's just that I can't. Not at the moment.' She could not tell him. If she did, he would attempt to be useful, override her decision, call in Scotland Yard – and ruin everything. Put Fanny in jeopardy, have police cars surrounding the house, alert Xavier. No – it was impossible. If he were here in person, if she could explain to him face-to-face . . .

'I'm sorry, David,' she said. 'I'm afraid you'll just have to trust me.'

'And if I don't?' She had guessed that he could be like this. Guessed from a certain hardness in his eyes, in unguarded moments, when he spoke of Caroline; from a tightening of the muscles around his mouth when he answered the telephone and Caroline's silvery laughter sounded along the wires. But he had never been like this with her before.

'Goodbye, David,' she said sadly, and replaced the receiver.

She went upstairs to bed, too tired for tears. All emotion drained finally from her by the events of the day. She had lost Fanny, she had found a murdered man and, now, it looked as though she had lost her husband.

But she was so tired, so exhausted. All she wanted to do was to sleep.

CHAPTER X

SHE WOKE to a sense of desolation that she could not at first understand, then remembrance came flooding back. Her watch said 7.00 but, when she drew back the curtains, the sun was high. She had, not surprisingly, forgotten to wind it before she went to bed this morning.

Downstairs, 1-2-3 (who would always be TIM to her) informed her that it was 10.30. She was only surprised that she hadn't slept longer – she felt as though she had had no sleep at all. Once awake, however, it was impossible to go back to sleep.

The kettle was boiling before she opened the door to bring in the milk. The three pints standing on the doorstep were like a dash of cold water in her face. What was she going to do with all that extra milk?

Numbly, she collected the bottles and brought them inside. Any helpful cookery book would, she realized, recommend a long session in the kitchen making puddings and custards – but cookery writers seldom foresaw the types of emergencies that were likely to leave one with a surplus of milk.

Over coffee and a buttered bun, she held a mental debate on the relative merits of cancelling the extra milk or allowing the deliveries to continue. At least it helped to keep her mind off the main problems. (Why hadn't Caroline telephoned? What was she up to now?)

She poured a second cup of coffee, still concentrating on all that extra milk. (It was much easier to worry about that than about David. What was he thinking – feeling – imagining – all those thousands of miles away?)

By noon, the telephone still hadn't rung. Zita checked it compulsively, every fifteen minutes or so, to make sure it was in working order. It was. No one was trying to contact her, that was all. (Where was Caroline? Was she trying to do something on her own? If she succeeded, would she remember that Zita was still anxiously awaiting developments and report her success? Or would she just assume that Zita would know – through some sort of telepathy – and go on about her own business? In that case, wouldn't Fanny make some protest – if only because she wanted her possessions back?)

Too many cups of coffee and too many cigarettes later, Zita was still asking herself the same pointless questions. She had no more idea of the correct answers than she had had when she first began asking them. (She tried to bury the other questions: Would David telephone again? Would he calm down and realize there must be a legitimate reason for her actions, or would he continue to think the worst? If so, would he come back at all?)

She was so absorbed in trying not to think about the latter questions that she did not, at first, register the sound of the afternoon post being pushed through the mail slot in the front door.

Then she moved quickly – there might just have been enough time, if he'd posted it as soon as he arrived, for a postcard to come from David. (Would he send another one – after last night?)

Three letters lay face up on the mat; her anxious steps slowed as she saw them. All had been mailed locally. Then something about the unfamiliar sprawling blue handwriting on one of the envelopes made her quicken her steps again. She stooped and picked up the letters, carrying them back into the lounge. She felt that she would rather be sitting down when she opened that envelope.

Without ever having seen her handwriting, she knew that the writing must be Fanny's. It was a child's and it was in the uniform American hand, varied only by the few personal touches the most determined teachers can't iron out. She realized that she was staring at the envelope in a daze, postponing the moment when she must open it. She took a deep breath and carefully levered the flap open. Very carefully, in case she destroyed some clues – but to whom could she show such clues? The police were out of it – had to be. And Caroline was not likely to be of any practical help.

Dear Zita,

Please to have my Mother by your telephone precisely 9.30 p.m. I will then be in contact with instructions. Please not to fail me.

Yours sinseerley,
Fanny.

It had been dictated, of course. Fanny had never shown any acquaintance with the word 'please'. Nor had she ever referred to Caroline as 'my mother', or by any name except Caroline. There was also the matter of the stilted, rather foreign phrasing.

Zita tried not to think about the blotches on the paper that might have been made by tears. An impatient kidnapper would not take kindly to having his English corrected by Fanny. (She hoped that was the only reason for the tears. Caroline might be confident that Xavier would not harm a child, but Zita had no such confidence.)

And where *was* Caroline now? Would she be here by 9.30 p.m.? If not, what would happen to Fanny? Would Xavier believe that she had no way to contact Caroline? Or would he think that Caroline was playing for time, hoping that he was bluffing? (What *did* kidnappers do with a victim the parent wouldn't ransom? It wasn't like an unredeemed pledge in a pawn shop – the child couldn't be offered to someone else.)

The letter had – Zita checked the date on the envelope – been posted yesterday. Presumably in the afternoon – before it had somehow become necessary to kill Melancholy. (Why? Because he protested at holding Fanny hostage? Because he wanted the child returned before they got the money back? Or was there another, more sinister, reason?)

Now that murder had been committed, everything was different. To use Xavier's own parlance, all bets were off. There might not be the promised telephone call tonight. Xavier might have left the country by now. (Taking Fanny with him? Or leaving her behind? Could he afford to leave a living witness behind? Was Fanny, even now – ?)

Inaction was maddening. Yet what was there she could effectively do? Until she had heard from Caroline, there was no possible action which might alleviate the situation. *If* she heard from Caroline.

Caroline, she argued with herself against a fresh onset of doubt, had promised to come today. Caroline had given her word. (But Caroline had given her word to many people, about many things. Caroline's word ceased to be binding the instant it inconvenienced Caroline.)

Zita carefully set Fanny's letter down on the sofa beside her and turned to the rest of the post, striving to maintain a semblance of normalcy, even though there was no one to witness it. At least, no witnesses that she was aware of. She glanced towards the bow window uneasily, but there were no watchers in the square. So far as she could see, the house was un-observed. That did not necessarily mean that there was not someone, somewhere – at the foot of the hill, behind a window in one of the houses across the way – watching to make sure that Caroline arrived to wait for her telephone message.

'Junk mail,' Zita's mind told her. Despite this, she was uncomfortable until she had shaken out the con-tents of the other two envelopes and proved herself right. One was an invitation to make a fortune by 'investing' in a Football Pool (should she pass it on to Caroline?); the other a strongly-worded suggestion that her life was incomplete if she did not take advantage of a marvellous new offer to purchase Breton-style cooking implements at only twice the price she would have to pay for them at her local shops. She tossed them into the wastepaper basket with relief. No further activity was called for on that score.

Her eyes fell on Fanny's letter again and she checked her watch: 2.00. Still no sign of Caroline. Had she planned to sail the boat back downriver, or to moor it somewhere and take a train to town? Would she come here directly, or go to her flat first and discover – ?

There was one way to find out. She pulled the telephone to her and dialled Caroline's number. It seemed to ring for an endless time at the other end, but Zita held on, knowing that Caroline – if she *were* there – would be doing some agonizing over whether or not to answer. Curiosity always won in the end, however.

Someone lifted the receiver.

'Hello?' Zita said.

There was no answer.

'Hello? Caroline? Is that you, Caroline?'

There was still no answer. There was not even the sound of breathing.

Abruptly, Zita had a grotesque vision of Melancholy, zombie-like, dragging himself from the bedroom to halt the ringing that was disturbing his final slumber.

She slammed the telephone down and found that she was trembling violently. Undoubtedly, Melancholy was on the move again, but not of his own volition. Had it been Xavier, come to see if Caroline had received his private message, who had lifted the phone? Or just one of his hirelings come to tidy up?

After a moment, she got up. A cup of tea might not help, but it wouldn't do any harm. She went into the kitchen and put the kettle on. Waiting for it to boil, she wandered aimlessly back to the living-room. She stood in the doorway and her eyes met the soft painted eyes of the dreamy portrait of Caroline hanging over the mantel. (Oh, Caroline, Caroline, if only you *were* like that. If dreaming were *all* you did, none of us would be in this mess now.)

Caroline came with the darkness, carrying a suitcase, slipping through the back door like a navy blue shadow. Zita closed the door behind her and leaned against it, feeling weak with relief. There had been so many times during this long day when she had thought that Caroline was not going to come at all.

'You took your time answering.' Caroline was her usual sweet self.

'I didn't hear you knocking at first.'

'What did you expect me to do – make enough noise to rouse the whole neighbourhood?' Caroline deposited her suitcase in a corner. '*Do* show some sense, Zita.' Coming from Caroline, it took one's breath away.

'Have you been to your flat today?'

'Of course not.' Caroline looked at her in surprise. 'Why should I have? You were going there last night to look for any message.' Her eyes narrowed with suspicion. 'You *did* go, didn't you?'

'Yes, I went,' Zita said grimly, abandoning any

thought of softening the blow for Caroline. 'And I found your message from Xavier. They'd moved Melancholy's body. He was lying in your bed.'

'No!' Caroline's eyes widened in terror as she absorbed the news. (Perhaps Xavier had not intended Caroline to call upon him for help. Perhaps the message had been the most obviously-read one: *You, too, could wind up dead.*)

'I don't believe it!' Caroline said.

'I wouldn't lie about a thing like that.' Zita controlled her voice carefully. Although Caroline was solid steel beneath that fluffy, doll-like exterior, even steel had a breaking point.

'No – ' Caroline raised a hand helplessly. 'No, I don't mean I don't believe *you*. I mean, it *can't* have been Xavier. He wouldn't *do* such a thing to *me*.'

'Perhaps he never thought you'd do what you've done to him,' Zita suggested softly, feeling a faint sympathy for Xavier. Anyone who knew Caroline for any length of time found that she eventually brought out their worst side.

'Oh, that!' Caroline brushed it aside, as she swept off her hat and shook out her hair. 'That's not the same sort of thing, at all.'

Zita stared at Caroline unbelievingly, less at what she had said than at what she had just revealed. The flawless maquillage was not surprising, Caroline naturally would not come to town looking as scruffy as she had been on the boat. But the other – those perfectly-arranged shining curls –

'You've been to the hairdresser!' Zita exclaimed

incredulously. Caroline's only child held hostage, alone, frightened, among strangers – and Caroline had calmly spent hours in a beauty salon getting the full treatment.

'Well, of course.' Caroline seemed surprised at her surprise. 'You don't think I'd get anywhere with Xavier looking less than my best, do you?'

'I suppose not,' Zita said slowly. It had never occurred to her before, but someone who depended upon her glamour for – let's face it – for her living, could not afford to let that glamour slip. Zita felt a sudden rush of gratitude for David, with whom one could relax and not worry that a smudge on the nose or laddered tights might set him thinking of greener pastures. (That is, her elation was sharply checked, if she still *had* David – after last night.)

'Come into the other room,' she told Caroline, hoping her tone was still civil. Whether Caroline meant to or not, she had a way of bruising every relationship she brushed against. Life had been so simple in the days B.C. – Before Caroline. But Before Caroline meant Before David, also.

'Such a *sweet* little house,' Caroline cooed, following Zita into the living-room. She had never been there before – it had been Zita's earnest hope that she might never have to invite Caroline into her home. Somehow, it had seemed that it would be less *her* home, once Caroline had trampled through it. Now that Caroline's footprints were all over her marriage, it hardly seemed to matter any more.

'I got this –' she handed Fanny's letter to Caroline – 'in the afternoon post.' She watched Caroline's cool expression change to one of consternation as she read it.

'But – ' Caroline lowered the letter, her voice was suddenly very small and frightened – 'but she's just a child – '

'I've been frantic for fear you wouldn't be here in time for that telephone call,' Zita said. 'Not that I'm at all sure that it will be made now. That letter must have been written and posted before Melancholy was killed. That may have changed all their plans.'

'But Fanny's a child – no more than a baby – ' Caroline wailed. 'They *can't* hurt her. They can't!'

'I hope not,' was as much comfort as Zita could offer.

'But – ' Caroline looked haunted – 'but – we've got to *do* something.'

It was that 'we' that annoyed Zita. Faced with the consequences of her own actions, Caroline still depended on everyone else to try to help her escape them.

'All we can do right now,' Zita said firmly, 'is wait and hope that we get that telephone call at 9.30. If we don't, then it will be time to try to think of something else to do.'

'I suppose you're right.' Caroline eyed her dubiously, as though suspecting – rightly – that Zita had still not completely abandoned the idea of calling in the police if the situation got any worse.

'Would you like a drink?' Zita crossed to the glass-fronted bookcase, the lower shelf of which was doubling as a drinks cabinet.

'Some brandy, if you have it,' Caroline agreed. She

stared absently at her own portrait over the mantel, but did not comment on it. She was still holding Fanny's letter.

'Here you are.' Zita gave Caroline her drink and, on second thought, poured one for herself. 'I notice – ' she probed delicately – 'you brought a suitcase.'

'Naturally.' Caroline turned wide eyes on her. 'You can't expect me to go back to the boat tonight. You needn't worry, I won't be any trouble. I can take Fanny's room. If she comes back tonight, she'll simply have to double-up with me.'

'I see,' Zita said faintly. Caroline, as usual, had everything planned to her own satisfaction. Whether it was to anyone else's or not didn't concern her.

'Now – ' Caroline finished her drink and stood up – 'if you'll show me to my room, I'll take my case up before it's time for that telephone call.'

CHAPTER XI

IT WAS PRECISELY 9.30 when the telephone rang.

Zita was a split-second ahead of Caroline in reaching for the telephone. Caroline hesitated, glaring, as though she would like to snatch the receiver from Zita's hand, but subsided.

'Hello?' Zita said, bracing herself for whatever demand or threat would come next. She held the receiver slightly away from her ear, to allow Caroline to hear, as well. 'Hello?'

'Zita . . .' After a long moment, the voice came over the wires, sounding puzzled. 'Is that you?'

'Yes,' she admitted guardedly, her voice low.

'You sound different,' he complained. 'Listen, darling, I'm sorry about last night. I lost my temper –'

'David!' she said. 'Oh, no!'

'Tell him to get off the line,' Caroline said urgently. 'You can't bother with him at a time like this.'

'What do you mean, "Oh, no"?' He was losing his temper again. 'Who's there with you? I can hear someone talking.'

'Darling, I'm sorry.' She pressed the receiver against her ear now, so that no sound could escape. 'I can't explain right now, but –' She could not hold a reconciliation scene with Caroline breathing down the back of her neck.

'David!' Caroline screamed towards the receiver.

'Hang up! We're expecting an important call. We can't talk to you right now.'

'Who *is* that?' David demanded. 'Why should I hang up?'

'It's Caroline,' Zita said desperately, 'and you shouldn't – That is, you should, but I'll ring back as soon as I can. What's your number?' She looked frantically for a pencil.

'What's Caroline doing there?' David asked, all his former suspicions flooding back into his voice. 'What are you two doing – getting your stories straight?'

'David, I –' She broke off as there was a sharp click and the dial tone. She stared incredulously at the pearly pink fingernails on the telephone cradle and raised her eyes to Caroline's face.

'You cut me off! I was having a private conversation with my husband – and you cut me off!'

'Well, he was *my* husband, too,' Caroline countered with the unforgivable, then backed away defensively. 'And I know what a bore he can be when he starts going on like that. He just goes on and on. It's the only way to stop him. You can patch it up with him later.'

'If there *is* a later,' Zita said grimly. At this rate, *she* would soon be referring to David in the past tense, too.

'Look at the time!' Caroline thrust her arm in front of Zita's face, turning her wrist to display her watch. 'It's three minutes past nine-thirty now. Xavier may have been trying to reach us already. What would he think if he found the line engaged?'

'He'd think –' she answered her own question, her voice rising in incipient hysteria – 'he'd think we were talking to the police. And what would happen to Fanny then?'

As they stared at each other, trying not to think of what might happen to Fanny, of what might have already happened to Fanny, the telephone rang anew.

'If that's David again –' Caroline said between clenched teeth.

They both lunged for the phone. This time Caroline won. 'Hello –?' she said tentatively, and stiffened. 'Yes . . . yes . . .' Unlike Zita, she did not hold the receiver in a way to encourage eavesdropping. She obviously intended her own conversation to be private.

'No –' Abruptly, Caroline balked. 'I'm not going to discuss it. I'm not going to say another word to you until I've spoken to Fanny. I want to be sure she's safe.'

The volume of sound, if not the exact words, reached Zita. Caroline blanched, but stood fast. 'It's no use your shouting,' she said. 'I want to talk to Fanny. Afterwards, I'll talk to you.'

There was a long silence, then Caroline's face warmed into animation. 'Fanny!' she cried. 'Fanny, darling! How are you, my sweet? Did they –? Yes . . . yes, she's here.'

Caroline held the phone out to Zita. 'Fanny wants,' she said coldly, 'to talk to *you*.'

'Zita? Zita?' Fanny's voice was bubbling excitedly.

'Zita, I've been kidnapped!' She sounded quite pleased about it, as though it were some kind of feather in her cap.

'Yes,' Zita said, 'I know.'

'Were you scared when you found I was gone? I wasn't scared at all.'

'Yes,' Zita admitted. 'I was scared.' It was as well Fanny was taking it this way.

'I thought you would be!' Fanny was triumphant. 'I'll bet Caroline wasn't scared, though, was she?'

'No,' Zita said, 'I don't believe she was. But – ' she modified hastily, 'she was upset. She was very upset.'

'Oh, that's just because she'll have to give the money back,' Fanny said casually. 'I knew she wouldn't be scared. I wasn't scared, either.'

'Fanny . . .' Zita said hesitantly. 'They're treating you well, aren't they?'

'They'd better.' Fanny was fiercely complacent. 'They're kidnappers – they can get the electric chair for this!'

'Fanny – don't say such things!' Zita was instantly terrified for the child. 'In any case – ' she tried for a calm, even tone lest her panic infect Fanny – 'that isn't true. We don't have the electric chair in England. We don't have a death penalty at all. It's been abolished.'

'Oh.' Fanny sounded subdued, either because of Zita's information or because of some overt threat in the background. 'Maybe I'd better watch my step, then.'

'Yes,' Zita said. 'I rather think you had.'

'What is it?' Caroline demanded urgently. 'What's she saying?'

'I think you ought to speak to your mother again,' Zita said. 'She *has* been worried about you.'

'Oh, okay.' Fanny gave a heavy sigh.

'Goodbye, then. Be a good girl and – ' Zita said, with an assurance she did not feel, 'we'll see you soon.'

'Zita – wait a minute. Don't go yet!' Abruptly, Fanny's bravado deserted her. 'Zita – ' a forlorn little voice wailed. 'Zita – I want to come back. I keep having nightmares here. And – and – Zita – I've lost Romeo.'

'No, you haven't,' Zita comforted quickly. 'We found him. Romeo's upstairs in your room, waiting for you.'

'Zita!' Caroline snatched the phone from her hand. 'I don't think *that* was wise!'

Belatedly, Zita remembered the circumstances in which they had found Romeo.

'Fanny, darling,' Caroline cooed desperately into the mouthpiece. 'Don't say anything more – and don't even mention Romeo again. Not until you're safely home. Do you understand?'

Mercifully, Fanny would not understand, not connect it with her nightmares, but it would be enough if she could just obey Caroline's instructions.

'That's lovely, Fanny,' Caroline said. 'All right . . .' her voice cooled. 'I'll speak to Xavier now.'

After that, it was evident that Xavier was doing most of the talking. Caroline simply listened, occasionally shaking her head wordlessly. After a few minutes, she broke into a low, keening moan – occasioned, Zita supposed, by the imminent prospect of having to part with her ill-gotten gains.

'No – ' Caroline interrupted in genuine anguish. 'No – I can't. I haven't – '

A whiplash roar cut across her protest. Caroline closed her eyes briefly and, when she opened them, silent tears began rolling down her face.

'Yes . . .' she murmured. 'I understand, Xavier. You – you didn't have to say that.'

Zita watched, suspended between compassion and a certain justifiable vindictiveness. It looked as though Caroline had met her match in Xavier. It was a shame that poor little Fanny had to be caught in the middle.

'No, please – ' Again Caroline tried to protest. 'Not tomorrow night. Can't we do it tonight? I – I want Fanny back *now*. I want her here with me tonight.'

Once more a rumbling tirade silenced her. It appeared that her wants had been considered for the last time.

'Yes,' Caroline said dully. 'I will. I . . . I promise.' Her hand was shaking as she replaced the receiver. She groped her way blindly to the sofa and sank down on it.

'Here.' Zita brought her a brandy. 'It's going to be all right now. It would have been worse if they'd changed their plans and not called. Once you've returned the – '

'No – ' Caroline choked. 'No, it's worse than ever. You don't know. You don't understand – '

'I don't?' Zita sat down carefully and studied Caroline. 'What else is there I don't know?'

'Ooooh.' Caroline sniffled and took a pull at the brandy. 'Haven't you got any Kleenex?'

Zita brought some silently and sat down.

'I suppose – ' Caroline looked up wistfully – 'I haven't been a very good mother. But you must admit – ' she pouted slightly – 'Fanny isn't a very lovable child.' In her tone was the grievance of a parent who felt herself shortchanged in being dealt an awkward child with a strong personality, rather than a docile, pink-and-white replica of herself.

'Fanny will get along,' Zita said, faintly surprised by the vehemence with which she rose to Fanny's defence. 'She's bright and she's tough. And there's still time for her to learn the social graces.' She hoped that that last statement was true. If Fanny didn't control her tongue, she might goad her kidnappers into throwing her into the Thames rather than returning her to her mother. Xavier had not seemed to possess a great deal of patience.

'I thought you were going to tell me something I didn't know,' Zita prodded, not too delicately. Caroline's confession of her deficiencies as a mother ranked in eyebrow-lifting qualities with the information that Queen Anne was dead.

'Oooh . . .' Caroline dipped into her brandy again. 'I just don't know *how* to tell you.'

'The money – ' Zita said. 'It was something about the money?' It hardly needed to be a question. Only money could bring out so much emotion in Caroline.

'Yes . . .' Caroline's tears began again. 'I don't know

what I'm going to do. It's too awful! What *can* I do?'

'Give it to him,' Zita said firmly. 'And get Fanny back.'

'That's just it,' Caroline wailed. 'I can't. I haven't got it.'

'What?' Zita found she was on her feet, standing over Caroline. It took a strong-minded effort not to begin shaking her. 'You must have it. What have you done with it?' Wild thoughts of numbered Swiss bank accounts rushed through her mind. (Had Caroline had time to get to Switzerland and hide the money? Perhaps where even *she* couldn't find it again? It was just the sort of thing she was capable of.)

'You *must* have the money,' Zita repeated desperately. 'You *took* it.'

'That's just it,' Caroline said. 'I did – but I didn't. And now I don't know what I'm going to do!'

'Explain that,' Zita said. 'Slowly and clearly. I'm not feeling very bright tonight.'

'Oh, do sit down!' Caroline glanced up impatiently. 'How can I think with you standing over me like some old schoolteacher?'

'All right.' Zita forced herself back into a chair. 'Now, explain.'

'Xavier gave me instructions,' Caroline said. 'I'm to pack the money in an old suitcase and leave it at the bottom of Wapping Old Stairs at high tide tomorrow night. Then, if everything's all right, I'll get Fanny back.'

'That sounds reasonable,' Zita said. It might have been a lot more awkward.

'But everything isn't all right.' Caroline drew a deep, unsteady breath. 'Then he said I wasn't to try anything funny. He wanted every penny of his money back. All £200,000 of it!' Her eyes were wild and pleading. 'And I haven't got it. I *told* you I didn't empty the safe. I left half. I only took £100,000 – ' Even now, she seemed to expect applause for her forbearance.

'If it was *all* missing, then someone else must have come along after me and taken it. But Xavier thinks I did it. And he'll never believe the truth! He said – he said, if I didn't return his £200,000, he'd – he'd – send Fanny back – piece by piece.

'He said – ' Caroline broke down completely – 'he said it would be a pleasure.'

They drank cup after cup of coffee in the kitchen because it didn't make any difference – neither of them could envisage sleeping tonight.

'Even if I could borrow the money somewhere,' Caroline said glumly, 'it still wouldn't be any good, because I'd never have a chance of ever paying it all back . . .'

Zita nodded; they had been over this ground before. She no longer bothered to wonder where Caroline thought she might borrow such a sum, particularly without security or without giving any reason for the loan. It seemed better to attack the problem from a more practical angle.

'Who else knew the combination of the safe?'

'Well . . .' Caroline appeared to be casting her mind

back into a past already becoming dim and distant to her. 'Xavier never actually *gave* anyone the combination – it was just one of those things we all knew.' Caroline's eyes slid sideways evasively. 'It wasn't hard to find out. Anyone at the club could have known.'

'Did he always keep that much money in it?' If so, it was a wonder he hadn't been robbed before. It was staggering to realize that Caroline had blandly walked away with as much as some bank robbers got from an armed raid. Perhaps she *did* deserve some credit for leaving half of it behind.

'No – at least, not for long. But he had the Bank Holiday takings in it. And I think he'd transferred some from somewhere else. There's been all sorts of talk lately about some trouble he'd been having with the Gaming Commission. I think they're trying to take his licence away. I don't know – ' she added virtuously. 'I don't pay much attention to that sort of thing.'

Except, Zita thought dryly, to know when the safe had the maximum amount in it.

'Tell me,' Zita said curiously. 'Even though you "only" took half his money, did you honestly think you could get away with it?'

'Really, Zita!' Caroline gave her an injured look. 'Xavier was never *mean* about money. I thought it would be ages before he noticed it was missing. And by that time, he couldn't be sure who'd taken it.' Her look unexpectedly turned sly. 'Anyway, he's in no position to complain about it.'

'No,' Zita said, 'I can see that.' If the Gaming Com-

mission and, presumably, the police were keeping an
eye on Xavier, he wouldn't wish to attract any more
attention. Especially as the money taken seemed to
be part of some gigantic income tax fiddle. The
American authorities had, she recalled, finally managed
to jail Al Capone on a charge of income tax evasion
when they were unable to get sufficient evidence on
the more serious offences they knew him to be guilty
of.

'It's too bad we can't tell the police,' Caroline said.
'It would serve him right to be sent to jail.'

He would not be the only one to go to jail, Zita
thought wistfully. She considered, for a moment,
whether a Caroline in Holloway could possibly be
more of an embarrassment than a Caroline constantly
in the gossip columns and consorting with unsavoury
gentlemen. Reluctantly, she decided that it could. For
one thing, Caroline would insist on being visited and
having errands run. David would be too soft-hearted
to refuse any plea from an incarcerated Caroline. For
that matter, Zita acknowledged ruefully, she had not
done a very good job of resisting Caroline's machinations herself.

'I'm not sure he *would* go to jail.' Zita pulled herself
together and tried to answer Caroline's last comment.
'They might just deport him instead.'

'Deport him!' Caroline's eyes blazed with hope. 'Do
you really think they might?'

'Not in time to do Fanny any good.' Zita brought
her back to earth rudely. Caroline had an infinite
capacity for losing track of problems she would rather

not think about. This time, she could not be allowed to get away with it. For Fanny's sake, she must be kept to the point.

(David had not called back. She must not allow herself to think about that. She had to keep to the point, too – for Fanny's sake.)

'You'll just have to give him back what money you did take, and hope that will calm him enough to make him listen to you about the rest,' Zita told Caroline. (Surely £100,000 would have a calming effect on anyone. Except, possibly, someone expecting £200,000.) 'Then, when he calls again, you can explain. He *must* return Fanny. He can't *want* to hurt a child.'

'Fanny's not a very lovable child,' Caroline said again. 'I – I thought I might take her in hand. Bring her over here to live with me for a while. When she was older – ' Caroline broke off, as though facing the fact for the first time that Fanny might not live to grow any older.

'I don't know what her father was thinking of to let her grow up so spoiled and selfish !' Caroline cried angrily. Once again, it was becoming someone else's fault – not Caroline's.

'What time is high tide tomorrow night ?' Zita asked wearily.

'*I* don't know.' Caroline looked surprised at being asked, as though her familiarity with boats couldn't be expected to extend to anything practical like tide tables.

'All right, we can find out. It ought to be in the evening paper.' She had tossed it, unread, on top of the pile of papers she would put out for the dustmen in the morning. She crossed to the pile now and retrieved it.

'What does it say?' Caroline's eyes lingered hungrily on the pile of newspapers before she turned to Zita.

'High tide: 10.35 p.m.'

'That gives us plenty of time,' Caroline exclaimed with satisfaction.

'Time for what? There's nothing we can do.' She did not view the hours stretching out ahead with the enthusiasm Caroline seemed to. 'Except wait.'

'We can think,' Caroline said. 'Perhaps we can come up with a plan.'

'We're too tired to think at all, right now,' Zita said. 'We ought to try to get some rest.'

'Yes,' Caroline said. 'But I'm *sure* I shan't sleep a wink, so – ' she swooped on the pile of newspapers and swept them up – 'I'll just take these up to my room and catch up with the news. I haven't seen a paper since I've been on that boat. I'm *days* behind with the news.'

'All right,' Zita said. Fraught though she was, she would probably manage a few hours sleep herself through sheer exhaustion. If Caroline had something to occupy her, it would keep her from seeking someone to talk to if she couldn't sleep.

'Good night.' Caroline made for the door. There had been, Zita noticed, no offer to help with the dishes.

'Tell me,' Zita said, just as Caroline was leaving the room. 'Did you think there wouldn't be *any* repercussions at all? If Xavier hadn't decided to kidnap

Fanny, he might still have found a way to send you to jail. Didn't you ever consider that?'

'Really, Zita.' Caroline turned in the doorway and drew herself up as much as her armload of papers would allow. 'You needn't take such a high-and-mighty tone with me, you know. If I go to jail, *you'll* be right in there with me.

'Just remember – ' she delivered her parting shot – 'you're an accessory after the fact!'

CHAPTER XII

CAROLINE DIDN'T SURFACE until four in the afternoon. Zita, who had fallen into an uneasy doze to the sound of paper rustling, was not entirely surprised. Waking at intervals between nightmares during a restless night, she had always been vaguely aware of paper still rustling. Caroline must have memorized every item in every newspaper before finally falling asleep.

'Just coffee, thank you,' Caroline said, in response to Zita's greeting. 'And perhaps some toast.'

Bringing the mug to the table, Zita found Caroline rubbing her hands and flexing her fingers thoughtfully.

'Something wrong with your hands?' she asked curiously.

'All those locks yesterday –' Caroline grasped the coffee mug eagerly, her fingers curling around it as though grateful for the heat. 'And I had to get through them all alone –' She looked at Zita accusingly. 'It's a wonder I have any skin left on my hands. And they're so stiff.'

'That *is* a shame.' Zita forebore to point out that, having been turfed off the boat to find her own way back to London, she could hardly be made to feel guilty because she hadn't been on deck to help poor Caroline. Nor could she be expected to have much sympathy.

'Oh, I'll be all right,' Caroline said, with a wan,

brave smile. She seemed to feel that something more was required. 'Really, Zita, this is awfully good coffee.'

'It's instant,' Zita said curtly. There was no justice. She knew that she looked haggard and hag-ridden, ten years older, with black circles under her eyes and a nerve in her forehead throbbing monotonously in the beginning of a headache. Whereas Caroline, who had had a great deal less sleep, merely looked pale and fragile, with a light violet staining under her eyes merely accentuating their colour and size. It appeared that having no conscience was as good as hours spent in a beauty salon.

'This toast is delicious, too.' Caroline had obviously decided it was expedient to expend some charm on her hostess. Zita eyed her suspiciously – what was she working towards now?

'And I *love* this little kitchen,' Caroline prattled on. 'Such a divine colour scheme . . .'

Zita poured a mug of coffee for herself and sat facing Caroline, but not listening to her. Pensively, she studied her husband's ex-wife. Could any ordinary woman – or man – ever understand a mind like that? Probably Caroline didn't herself. But she didn't need to, she existed on a different plane, caring only for the whim of the moment. Was it entirely fortuitous that, in most cases, the whim also possessed large sums of money to lavish on her?

Perhaps Caroline would have seemed more in her element if she had been born into a different place and different century. A French courtesan at the Court

of the Sun King? Or a harem favourite of some sheik
or sultan?

No. No – Caroline wouldn't have lasted ten minutes
in a harem. For any one of the shoddy little episodes
that had left David so wounded and untrusting, any
sultan worth his salt would have exacted an immediate
and terrible revenge. Caroline would have been strung
up over a camp fire, an incision made with a curved
scimitar, one end of her intestines tied to the saddle of
a half-wild Arabian stallion and . . .

'That's the first time I've seen you smile in *days*!'
Caroline exclaimed. 'I'm *so* glad we're friends again!'

'More coffee?' Zita offered guiltily.

'I'd love some more!' Caroline leaned forward,
elbows on table, massaging her fingers absently. 'Oh,
Zita, now I feel I can ask you. You *will* come with me
tonight, won't you?'

'Tonight?' Zita set her mug down sharply, a small
tidal wave of coffee slopped on to the table.

'Xavier didn't *say* I was to come alone,' Caroline
pointed out. 'In fact,' she added righteously, 'he
couldn't have expected me to. *Not* in a district like
that.'

Caroline's face and tone were obviously trying to
project images of a helpless waif brutally seized and
ravished by lustful denizens of the East End. The
expression Caroline actually succeeded in producing
was one of mild dismay. Probably occasioned by the
thought that anyone who had to resort to raping her
must have an empty wallet.

'Please, Zita,' Caroline wheedled. 'We can go and have a nice dinner somewhere. Then we can take a taxi to the town of Ramsgate and have a drink there until it's high tide. That's right by Wapping Old Stairs, so we won't have to be wandering about on our own.' Caroline fluttered her eyelashes wistfully. 'Say you'll come with me.'

Zita wished, with irritation, that Caroline could understand that her little coquetries didn't work with another woman. Or perhaps – she tried to be fair – they were so much a part of Caroline that she didn't even realize she was using them.

'What about Fanny? Suppose they bring her back here while you're delivering the money? They'd find an empty house – locked – '

'Oh, Xavier wouldn't do *that*,' Caroline said. 'I know him. He'll have Fanny there to make the exchange. He won't want to hang around London long after he gets the money. He'd been talking about something frightfully important he had to do on the Continent. I'm really surprised – ' once more, grievance throbbed in her voice – 'that he postponed his trip just because of the money. I didn't expect him to.'

'Perhaps,' Zita suggested caustically, 'he got big by bothering.' Nevertheless, there was probably something in what Caroline had said. Xavier wouldn't want to be burdened by a small child any longer than was strictly necessary. They might find Fanny sitting at the top of Wapping Old Stairs when they deposited the suit-case with the money. In which case, it might be more reassuring to Fanny, after her ordeal, to be met by two people she knew.

'We'll eat here,' Zita decided. 'And I don't see how we can go into that pub carrying a suitcase without attracting too much attention. We'll give it as the address to the taxi driver, but we won't go inside.'

'Oh, good,' Caroline said. 'I *knew* you'd see it my way.' She sighed happily, flexing her fingers. 'It's *so* nice to be friends again.'

Zita studied her thoughtfully. She had the uneasy feeling that, in some way, Caroline had put something over on her again. But what? She sighed, too, *not* happily.

Anyone who had Caroline for a friend didn't need any enemies.

A clock somewhere was chiming ten as the taxi set them down outside the town of Ramsgate.

'Time for a quick one before closing,' the driver said cheekily. 'Or – ' he eyed the suitcase – 'are you meeting a friend and going on?'

Tight-lipped, Zita paid the fare and tipped rather less than she had intended, while Caroline stood to one side, smiling vaguely.

The taxi was in no hurry about moving off, and Zita had to rummage about in her handbag, as though she were looking for something she must find before they entered the pub.

A man and a woman emerged from the pub in a gust of light, warmth and noise, and hailed the taxi with delight. They got in and it moved off slowly, the driver casting a final curious look backwards. He would remember them – at least, for a short time – but was it likely to be of any importance?

There was another burst of laughter and jollity from inside the pub, obviously portending another departure. Silently, Zita and Caroline moved away, starting down the passageway that led to the top of Wapping Old Stairs. It was clean and well lit, not at all what might have been expected, side entrances to the pub opened on to it. It was also very short.

'This can't be right!' Caroline stopped aghast. 'It *can't* be!'

Just beyond the pub, they had reached the end of the passage, their way barred by vertical iron railings. A chain and padlock looked as though they had not been disturbed for years.

'It can't be right,' Caroline said again.

'It's Wapping Old Stairs,' Zita pointed out. Two steps led up to the iron railing and, beyond it, the flight of stairs continued down to the river.

The river was dark and swift. Many bodies – or pieces of them – had fetched up on Wapping Old Stairs and the stretch of mud and shale left immediately below them by low tide. Along this reach of the river, there had once stood a gallows tree, suspending an iron cage in which hanged pirates and murderers were displayed as a grim warning to others contemplating the same path. It would not be surprising if ghosts of these dead criminals haunted this place and the dark surrounding alleys. On a night like this, it would be an easy thing to believe.

It had begun to rain, a soft drizzle which gave every

promise of developing into a full downpour before long.

'But – how can we leave the money *here*?' Caroline wailed. 'Where *is* he? What time is it?'

Zita dealt with the question she felt she could best cope with. She looked at her watch and incredulously held it up to her ear. It was still ticking. 'Three minutes past ten,' she said. They seemed to have been here for an hour.

'Is that all?' Caroline stared out into the mist rising from the river, then turned and looked down the passageway leading back to the street. Both vicinities were equally deserted. 'Where is he? Why isn't he here? What are we supposed to do now?'

'What were the precise instructions?' Zita asked a more practical question. 'Are we supposed to wait? Or do we leave the – the suitcase here and go away?' She had nearly said 'money', but felt, more discreetly than Caroline, that it was not a word to be uttered aloud in these circumstances and in these surroundings.

'He didn't say exactly.' Caroline sounded uncertain. 'He said something about the bottom of the stairs – but I'd call this the top. And we can't get to the bottom – the way is barred.' Caroline's voice began to quiver. 'He's done it deliberately – just to upset me.'

The lights in the passageway seemed to dim, probably the effect of the increasing mist. Several people emerged from the saloon bar, a couple of them hesitated to cast curious glances at the two women loitering at the end of the passageway. It would not be a good idea to remain where they were for much longer.

They were in no position to face anyone who might demand an explanation of their continued presence.

'He *can't* mean us just to leave it here,' Caroline said. '*Anyone* might come along and pick it up. And then he'd never believe we'd left it at all, and Fanny – '

'Yes,' Zita said quickly. Realization seemed to sweep over Caroline at odd moments, and tears would do no good right now. 'We'd better wait a while longer and see what happens.'

'But . . . how *much* longer?' Caroline was not to be comforted.

Zita shrugged, knowing as well as Caroline how very conspicuous they were going to be after the pub had let out. Of course, Xavier might be intending to meet them at the closing hour, so that the melée of people milling about would cover the transfer of the suitcase. On the other hand, why should he worry about cover? He was not some anonymous kidnapper. They not only knew his name – it was, in fact, his own money he was trying to retrieve.

Another five minutes ticked endlessly past, during which the rain thickened, the lights grew dimmer still, and the Thames lapped hungrily at the lower end of Wapping Old Stairs. Instinctively, Zita found herself paying more attention to the river. It would be easy now for a rowboat to come up against the steps, a dark figure to mount the stairs – then the suitcase could be handed over the railings, which would provide the figure with protection against being followed. Fanny could be delivered later – might even now be waiting at home for them.

It would be a workable procedure and very simple. Where was Xavier's yacht normally moored? Caroline had never said.

'Oh, I can't stand much more of this!' Caroline began to prowl restlessly, keeping to the side of the pasageway opposite the pub as though shrinking from the noise and merriment inside.

At first, Caroline just walked down a few paces, then turned and walked back. Gradually, the distance she covered grew longer, until she reached the end of the passageway before each turn, pausing to look down the street before resuming her circuit. Even in her prowling, Zita noticed, with what would under other circumstances be amusement, she kept the suitcase clutched tightly in her grasp.

Although equally uneasy, Zita kept a vigil at the gate of Wapping Old Stairs, still expecting to be accosted with whispered instructions through the bars at any moment.

Her attention was still on the river when there came a muffled shriek from Caroline.

'Caroline – ?' Zita turned and sped down the passageway to the street, coming up behind Caroline just in time to see the dark figure wrestling for the suitcase.

'It isn't fair – ' Caroline gasped, as the suitcase was wrenched from her. 'Fanny? Where's Fanny? You promised – '

A dark limp bundle was thrust into her arms and the tall figure melted away into the night, taking the suitcase with him.

'Fanny.' Zita turned back the bit of blanket sheltering Fanny's head. 'Fanny, it's all right. We're here.'

'Fanny, darling,' Caroline cried. 'You're safe now. You're with Mummy again.'

Fanny didn't answer.

'Fanny – ?' They carried her into the glow of a streetlamp. She was breathing lightly and shallowly, eyes closed, traces of tearstains on her face.

'Fanny.' Caroline shook her gently. 'Wake up, darling. Everything is all right now.'

Fanny didn't stir.

'They've given her something to keep her quiet,' Zita diagnosed. 'We'd better get her home and call a doctor.'

As it was so near to closing time, a taxi cruised down the street hopefully. Zita hailed it.

'Yes,' Caroline said dubiously. 'I suppose we ought to.'

Zita carefully set Fanny down on the sofa, while Caroline stood by uneasily. Fanny appeared to be sleeping more normally now, but it was best not to take chances. She straightened up and reached for the telephone.

'Oh no.' Caroline was there before her. 'No, I'm sure that won't be necessary. Fanny's a lot better already. Just look at her. She'll be all right by morning.'

'Just the same – ' Zita tried to sidestep Caroline, but Caroline moved, too – 'we ought to have the doctor.'

'No, really,' Caroline protested. 'What would we tell a doctor? It would be so awkward – '

Zita hesitated, loathing to admit that Caroline was

right. A doctor could hardly be presented with a drugged child without demanding some sort of explanation.

'Xavier knows what he's doing.' Caroline pressed home the advantage she sensed. 'He's always very careful. He wouldn't have given Fanny too much – '

Fanny stirred and moaned faintly, as though recognizing her name and trying to react to it.

'See – ' Caroline said triumphantly. 'There's nothing to worry about.'

Zita checked again. Fanny wasn't running a temperature and her pulse seemed strong, although still sluggish. It was probably true that she would be back to normal by morning.

'Besides,' Caroline said. 'We haven't time.'

'What?' Zita turned, but Caroline had left the room and was climbing the stairs to the bedroom she and Fanny were to share. Leaving Zita, once again, to carry Fanny, who was not the lightweight she looked.

Zita bent and gathered Fanny up, trying to disturb her as little as possible, although it was unlikely that anything would waken her before morning. At the foot of the stairs, she met Caroline, coming down – and carrying another suitcase.

'You've been awfully kind, Zita,' Caroline said, in a valedictory way. 'But we mustn't impose on your good nature any longer. We must be going now – and thank you for everything.'

'Going where?' Zita asked blankly, unable to believe either her eyes or her ears. Caroline *couldn't* intend to take Fanny away in this state.

'Oh, don't worry.' Caroline gestured airily with a letter she held in her other hand. 'We'll be all right.'

'I'm sure *you* will be,' Zita said grimly. 'But what about Fanny?'

'*What* about her?' Caroline drew herself up. 'She'll be safer with me than with you. After all, we wouldn't have had all this trouble if you hadn't let her be taken away from you in the first place.'

'The *first* place,' Zita reminded, 'was when you made off with Xavier's money. Without that, nothing else would have happened.'

'There you go again – ' Caroline continued down the stairs, forcing Zita to step back and then sweeping past her. 'Always finding fault!'

'It's pouring outside.' Zita followed her into the living-room. 'You can't take Fanny out in this. She may be all right now, but her resistance will be lowered. She's liable to catch pneumonia – '

'Really, Zita,' Caroline sighed. 'You *do* go on so.' She noticed Zita looking at the envelope in her hand and pointedly turned it round so that the address didn't show. 'I can't leave her here. Have you forgotten? Xavier wanted £200,000 – and he didn't get it.'

Caroline's mouth tightened. 'I locked the suitcase so, with luck, it will take him quite a while to open it. But when he finds out, he'll come looking for me and Fanny – ' She broke off abruptly.

'And find *me* here – alone.' Zita finished the sentence Caroline had obviously thought better of finishing.

'Well, you can come with us, if you like,' Caroline offered half-heartedly.

'Thank you, no,' Zita said. She felt that she would prefer to face an enraged Xavier than to spend any more time in Caroline's company. She deposited Fanny on the sofa again and stood looking down at her thoughtfully.

'But you do see that we must go,' Caroline insisted.

'And suppose Fanny *isn't* all right in the morning? What could you do? Somewhere along the river, knowing nothing about the next town, nor where you could find a doctor.'

As usual, Caroline was acting without thinking the situation through. If it were only Caroline at risk, the temptation would be strong to let her go and sort out her own destiny. But Fanny was involved. As Caroline always managed to involve the innocent in her machinations. They were the ones who were inevitably hurt while Caroline danced away unscathed to new places, new adventures – and to deliver more wounds to new and unsuspecting friends.

'You *do* fuss so,' Caroline pouted. 'Why must you always look on the dark side? Fanny isn't going to catch pneumonia, she won't develop complications, and we aren't going to need a doctor in a hurry. I don't see why you have to dramatize everything.'

'Her doll,' Zita said, employing delaying tactics. The drumming rain was slashing against the windows, getting worse by the minute. Surely, even Caroline would think twice about going out again into a night like this.

'I promised her we had Romeo safe for her. She'll be upset if she doesn't see him when she wakens.'

Before Caroline could protest, Zita left the room, hurrying up the stairs to Fanny's bedroom. Traces of Caroline's cyclonic packing were everywhere – drawers not shut, cupboard door swinging open, a tracery of newspaper confetti outlining the waste-basket, a tiny crumpled sock lying forlornly beside the bed. And, lying against the pillows, Romeo, his soft dark eyes under the extravagant lashes seeming to greet her. She caught him up and rushed downstairs again.

'I don't see how I can manage that,' Caroline said crossly. 'I'll have quite enough to carry, what with Fanny and the suitcase. You shouldn't have bothered.'

Fanny's arms closed round Romeo, though she still didn't waken. A faint smile slid across her lips, she seemed to know that he was there, bringing some sort of reassurance. It had been worth bothering about.

'You can't possibly manage it all,' Zita agreed. 'Why don't you leave the suitcase and let me bring it to you –'

She broke off. Caroline had drawn back with a strange expression, as though she found the suggestion abhorrent – or frightening.

'No!' she said. 'No, Zita, thank you – but that's quite impossible. There – there are things in it I need. To-night.'

'What things?' A slow suspicion began to grow at the back of Zita's mind. 'You're very well equipped on the boat. You have everything you need, and one more night without pyjamas isn't going to make much difference to Fanny at this stage.'

'Zita, stop hounding me!' Caroline's voice rose precipitously. 'I won't have it! We're leaving *now* – and that's all there is to it.'

She gathered Fanny up clumsily, trying to counterbalance her against the suitcase. Romeo fell to the floor and Fanny let out a fretful moan, twisting restlessly. Zita picked Romeo up.

'Just open the door for me,' Caroline ordered. 'And don't say another word.'

Zita opened the door, humouring her as she would have humoured Fanny herself in one of her childish rages. She would follow behind until Caroline found a taxi, or until she realized how hopeless it was and was ready to return sensibly to the house.

Caroline shifted Fanny against her shoulder, took a better grip on the suitcase, and started out of the door. On the step, she halted abruptly, then backed slowly into the hall again.

'Now see what you've done,' she accused Zita bitterly. 'It's too late!'

CHAPTER XIII

THE MAN followed Caroline into the hallway. Like so many of the famous – and notorious – he was a lot shorter than he looked in photographs. And deadlier. He was carrying the twin to Caroline's suitcase. Caroline continued to back away from his rage.

'You bitch!' he said. The greeting was succinct, but sincere. 'You lying, thieving, cheating, double-crossing bitch!'

It was also, Zita thought, an excellent assessment of Caroline, although a trifle on the mild side. Despite a fairly sheltered upbringing, she could think of several more pungent descriptive phrases for Caroline, herself. She followed them into the living-room, pausing only to shut the front door.

Caroline had dumped Fanny back on the sofa and moved to put the sofa between herself and Xavier. She was still clutching the suitcase.

'What have you done to Fanny?' Caroline always seemed to operate on the theory that attack is the best defence. She hurled the question accusingly at Xavier now. 'She *still* hasn't woken up.'

'Forget the kid.' Xavier barely glanced at Fanny. 'This is between *us*.'

'Please don't raise your voice.' Caroline came out from behind the sofa. She was now minus the suitcase. 'Sit down and have a drink. I'm sure we can discuss this like civilized people.'

Caroline had obviously discovered that the best way to handle Xavier was with sheer effrontery. Perhaps that was the secret of her success with most people. Xavier sat down, staring at her.

'That's better.' Caroline crossed to the drinks cabinet and began pouring. She didn't ask what anyone wanted, simply brought out the decanter, handed brandy around impartially, and retreated with her own glass to pose beneath the portrait of herself.

Zita discovered she was still clutching Romeo. She replaced him in Fanny's arms and, moving Fanny to one side, sat down on the sofa with her. For the first time, Xavier seemed aware of her existence. He looked at her curiously.

'Who are you?'

'This is my house,' Zita said faintly. She looked at Caroline, standing beneath her own portrait and looking very much the chatelaine. She wished now that she had lit the gas fire when she came in – Caroline would not be able to pose there so prettily with the backs of her legs scorching.

'This is my house,' Zita repeated, more firmly, not quite sure who she was trying to convince.

'We're sort of related,' Caroline brushed off the inquiry.

Xavier raised an eyebrow. 'I didn't know you had any relatives.'

'I married her ex-husband,' Zita said. '*One* of her ex-husbands.'

'The artist one.' Xavier looked up at the portrait

and nodded. 'To her, that makes you practically sisters.' He seemed satisfied with the explanation. 'What are you getting out of this?'

'A headache,' Zita said truthfully.

'Yeah,' Xavier nodded. 'She gets me that way, too, sometimes.'

'It isn't very *nice* of you two,' Caroline pouted, 'to talk about me as though I weren't here.'

She had gone too far. She should not have brought attention back to herself. Xavier's eyes narrowed and hardened. '*You* talk about "nice"!' he exploded. 'You think thieving's nice?'

'You needn't be rude –' Caroline began.

'No.' He held up his hand. 'No more talking. Just give me my money.'

'She doesn't have it.' Zita felt compelled to intervene. Caroline, unusually, appeared to have been stricken dumb – perhaps by the knowledge that Xavier would no longer believe anything she said. She had overdrawn on the bank of his tolerance and affection – and the time for an accounting had come.

'What do you mean?' Xavier turned to stare at her. His eyes passed curiously over the doll in Fanny's arms. 'That's funny,' he said. 'I thought the kid lost that. She was whining about it all one night.' He shrugged, dismissing it. 'Just another little liar – like her mother.'

Zita stiffened, then relaxed. Evidently, Xavier did not realize *where* Fanny had lost the doll. The memory of that place was a reminder that Xavier was far deadlier and more vicious than he appeared.

'What do you mean, she doesn't have the money?'
Caroline still had not spoken and he returned to the
point. 'She's got it, all right – don't let her fool you.'

'She didn't take as much as you thought,' Zita said.
'She left half of it in the safe. If that's gone, then
someone else must have taken it. She gave you all she
had.'

'You think so?' A cold spasm that might have been
meant as a smile twisted his mouth.

'Yes,' Zita said. She met his eyes, willing him to be
convinced.

'She told you that, did she?' He shook his head,
almost in admiration. 'And you believed her?'

'Yes, of course. Why shouldn't I? She wouldn't
play games with her child's life at stake. Money isn't
worth it.'

'You're a nice lady.' Xavier nodded. 'Your husband
struck it lucky – the second time. Now, I show you
something.'

He bent down to unfasten the twisted catches of the
suitcase at his feet and swung the cover back.

Zita gasped, she had never seen so much money
before. The tidy little packets, sorted into denomina-
tions, filled the suitcase to the brim.

'Nice, eh?' Xavier looked to her for agreement.
'Lots of money, eh? Now I show you something else.'

Leaning down again, he neatly stripped the top bill
from each pile. Zita gasped again, a leaden feeling of
despair and defeat settled upon her.

'Oh, Caroline,' she said. 'How *could* you?'

The elastic bands now held tidy packets of newspaper cut to the size of the genuine top bill. *That* was what Caroline had been doing, rustling newspapers far into the night. But . . . with Fanny's safety in the balance – Fanny, who was being held hostage for the safe return of the money.

'Oh, Caroline!' she said again.

'Nice relative you got, eh, lady?' Xavier smiled grimly.

'No wonder your hands were sore this morning,' Zita said.

'It wasn't easy, cutting all that out with just my manicure scissors and Fanny's paper doll scissors.' Caroline massaged her fingers in a mute appeal for sympathy.

'I didn't feel I could ask you to help. I must say, Zita, you've been a great disappointment to me. I'd always thought of you as someone I could depend on.' She frowned. 'But you're no help at all.'

Zita decided to ignore this. She had never before appreciated the immense self-restraint practised by Caroline's ex-husbands in merely divorcing her, rather than murdering her. Even Xavier seemed to have an iron control – although Caroline was obviously determined to push her luck.

'I'll take my money,' he ordered. 'Now!'

Caroline didn't move. She might not have heard the order – or the dangerous note in his voice – so unconcerned did she appear. Xavier began to rise.

'I'll get it,' Zita said hastily. 'It will be in her suitcase.' The suitcase Caroline could not be parted from – because it contained something so essential to her.

It could only be money.

'Traitor!' Caroline sneered. 'And you're scared, too.' For an instant, it was a disconcerting echo of Fanny.

'She's got more sense than you have,' Xavier said. 'And that wouldn't be hard.'

The letter Caroline had been intending to post was lying face down on top of the suitcase. Zita picked it up before lifting the suitcase and bringing it round to place before Xavier.

'It's locked – ' Caroline came fluttering forward. 'And I – I've lost the key.'

'That's too bad,' Xavier said. 'We'll have to see what we can do without a key.' He clenched his fist and delivered a couple of expert punches on either side of the lock. It sprang open.

'Ohhh, noooo,' Caroline moaned. She seemed to be actively suffering.

'There!' Xavier flipped open the lid and displayed the neat stacks of Treasury notes inside. 'She doesn't have the money, eh?'

'Caroline . . .' Zita grieved. 'And I believed you.'

'It's true,' Caroline protested, with increasing agitation. 'I only took half, I swear to you.'

'So,' Xavier said. 'Now we count it.' He pulled out a stack of five-pound notes and began to rifle through them expertly. Then he put the stack to one side and took up another. It was obvious that it wouldn't take him long to count it all. He would have made an excellent bank clerk – had he opted for honesty.

Zita resumed her seat beside Fanny. Noticing that she was still holding Caroline's letter, she set it down beside Fanny, not even curious enough to glance at the address. Knowing the way Caroline's mind worked, the key to the suitcase was probably inside, addressed to herself at some accommodation address where she could pick it up later.

Caroline still fluttered nervously around Xavier's chair – a moth drawn irresistibly by the incandescence of the piles of money he was handling.

Xavier ignored her, concentrating, as she was, only on the money. When he did look up, it was to frown. 'Where's the rest of it?' he demanded. 'There's only a hundred thousand here.'

'That's what we've been trying to tell you,' Caroline said. 'That's all I took. I left the rest for you. Someone else must have taken it. You should be looking for them – not me.'

'I should, eh?' He stared at her reflectively. 'You double-crossed me before, you've just tried to double-cross me now. Why should I believe a word you say?'

'Because it's true,' Caroline wailed.

'True!' Xavier looked pointedly at the suitcase filled with chopped newsprint. 'Like it was true you were returning me the other hundred thousand in that suitcase?'

'I can explain that – ' Caroline insisted desperately. She advanced and retreated on Xavier's chair. It was, Zita thought with sudden anxiety, very much like the broken-wing deception with which a wild bird lures the hunters into chasing her and away from the nest and nestlings.

But Fanny was already safe. Xavier had not threatened her by word or gesture since he had arrived. Zita found that she now believed Caroline's earlier statement that Xavier would not harm a child. Why, indeed, should he pay any more attention to the child, when it had been the mother he was seeking and she was here with him now? No, Caroline was not trying to protect Fanny. She had some other reason for wanting his attention distracted – focused on her and not on someone or something over on his right. Zita looked around thoughtfully, her uneasiness increasing. Caroline was up to no good again – her behaviour bore all the earmarks of it. But what was it this time?

'If you think you can explain *that* away – ' Xavier indicated the bundles of dummy currency – 'I'd be very interested to hear your explanation.'

'If you're going to be like that about it – ' Caroline moved huffily towards her portrait again – 'I shan't bother.'

'Oh yes, you will.' Xavier stood and advanced upon her. Once again, he seemed menacing.

'You've closed your mind against me,' Caroline accused. 'You aren't willing to see things my way at all – '

'For heaven's sake, Caroline,' Zita interrupted. 'If you won't tell him, at least tell *me*. I think you owe me some sort of explanation. *Why* did you try to keep back his money?'

'Well, because – ' Caroline faced Zita, widening her eyes innocently. 'Because he asked for too much. I simply didn't *have* all that – and he'd never have believed I didn't. So, since I couldn't give him all he wanted, I thought . . .' She faltered to a stop, obviously thrown off-stride by the dumbfounded look on Zita's face.

'You thought you might as well be hung for a sheep as a lamb,' Zita finished. There was no use, she knew, in appealing to Caroline's sense of decency, maternal instincts, or any other non-profit-making reactions other women came into this world equipped with.

'There you go again,' Caroline stormed. 'Nagging and complaining! And it's all your fault, anyway. If you hadn't shallied about and wasted time and delayed me, Fanny and I would have been gone by now and everything would be all right. We'd have been miles away before – ' She broke off, remembering belatedly that Xavier was standing beside her listening with great interest to every word.

'Let's get one thing straight, eh?' he said. 'You wouldn't have got away. That dumb, I'm not. There's a watch on this house. There has been from the beginning. Wherever you went, Melancholy would have followed you and reported to me later.'

Melancholy. Zita and Caroline exchanged stricken glances, their precarious alliance snapping into full force again. The sudden silence twanged through the room like a broken violin string. Zita was aware that both she and Caroline had frozen like foxes run to earth, but she was unable to move and break the spell.

'So,' Xavier said softly. 'Perhaps there is something else one of you charming ladies might like to tell me, eh?'

'Oh no,' Caroline said quickly. 'We've told you

everything we know.'

'That's *your* story.' Xavier dismissed her and turned to Zita. 'What's yours?'

'Mine? I have no story. I mean, I don't know – ' Zita found herself on her feet, moving to one side. Suddenly, it was important to her, too, to keep attention away from Fanny. 'I don't know what you're talking about.'

'You don't, eh?' Xavier glanced at her, then, more sharply, at a patch of white on the carpet.

The envelope. Caroline's letter. On the sofa, it had been half hidden by Zita's skirt. When Zita surged to her feet so swiftly, it had flipped to the floor – address side up.

Caroline gasped and looked as though she were about to faint.

'Well, well, well.' Xavier moved forward un-hurriedly, bent and retrieved the envelope. He studied it thoughtfully for a moment before raising his head to inquire, 'And who has been writing letters to Scotland Yard?'

CHAPTER XIV

CAROLINE REMAINED SILENT, her eyes filled with tears, her expression would have moved a heart of stone. Unfortunately, it didn't work on anyone who knew her.

'Dirty, double-crossing little bitch!' Xavier raised his hand and Caroline flinched.

'No.' He lowered the hand again. 'I lay one finger on you and I won't be able to stop. I've never killed a woman – yet.' He went back to his chair and sat down. 'You want to tell me what it says, or you want me to guess?'

'Oh, Caroline,' Zita said weakly. She returned to the sofa and sank on to it, feeling that her legs would no longer hold her up. 'Caroline, Caroline.'

'There you go again,' Caroline pouted. 'And you were the one who gave me the idea.'

'*I* gave it to you? I never – '

'Yes, you did,' Caroline insisted. 'You said maybe they'd deport Xavier. And I realized that would solve everything. And they *would* – if only they knew half the things he'd been doing, and where to find the evidence . . . And so . . .'

'And so!' Xavier said, with soft finality. He slid his thumb under the flap and opened the envelope. There were several sheets of paper inside, bulky with the carefully cut out words and letters pasted to them.

He gave Caroline one piercing look and began reading.

Caroline shrugged and returned to the drinks cabinet. She poured fresh drinks all round. She had regained some of her colour and Zita felt, with some dismay, that she was already planning something else.

'You knew about *that*, eh?' Xavier said absently, turning a page. '*And* that?' He glanced upwards sharply. 'I double-parked on a yellow line six months ago – how did you miss it?'

He was taking it awfully well, Zita thought. Of course, having safely intercepted the letter, he could afford to be amused.

With the final two pages, his face changed – hardened and turned cold. Tight-lipped, he read them, then turned back and read them again.

'What you think you're pulling?' Caroline backed away from the growing fury in his face. 'The other things you accuse me – okay. But *this* –' He waved the final pages. 'How you think you get away with a lie like this?'

'It's true,' Caroline said faintly. She turned to Zita. 'Tell him it's the truth.'

'What is?' Zita twisted her head, trying to get a glimpse of the unevenly chopped and pasted letter-print on the pages. 'I don't know what you're talking about,' she disclaimed, without any real hope. There could be only one subject that could infuriate Xavier and terrify Caroline quite so much.

'Melancholy!' Xavier confirmed her guess. 'This lying little bitch is trying to tell the cops I killed Melancholy. Melancholy – my best friend! My business partner. My – '

'He's dead,' Caroline said.

'He is not!' Xavier glared at her.

'We found the body.' Zita backed Caroline reluctantly. 'He'd been stabbed.'

'No!'

'I found the body – twice,' Zita said. 'There's no doubt about it. He was dead.'

'You crazy – both of you!' Xavier looked from one to the other. 'Why do you try to tell me these things? What trick is she – ' he jerked his head at Caroline – 'plotting now?'

'There's no trick.' Zita met his gaze evenly. 'There was a dead man in the river cottage when we went there two nights ago. Later that night, I saw him again – he'd been moved to Caroline's flat.'

'Two nights ago?' Xavier laughed – there seemed to be a trace of relief in his laughter. 'Now I know you lie. Melancholy has been watching this house, reporting to me. I heard from him just a few hours ago, when you left to bring me the suitcase. He is alive.'

'There *was* a dead man,' Zita insisted. 'Of course – ' A sudden mistrust of Caroline swamped her. 'I don't know *who* he was. Caroline identified him.'

'It *was* Melancholy,' Caroline said. 'Why don't you ever believe anything I say?' Her complaint was becoming automatic, as though she had lost interest in the proceedings. Her eyes, which had been focused on the suitcase full of money, switched briefly to Zita's face, to Xavier's, then returned to rest on the stacks of currency with hopeless longing.

Fanny moaned and stirred. Zita turned to her, but she was still asleep, although seemingly nearer the threshold of consciousness.

'Because you're a liar,' Xavier answered Caroline's plaint. 'Who can believe anything a liar says? Not on a stack of Bibles would I trust your word.' Yet Xavier had begun to sound faintly uncertain, a thoughtful frown began to deepen on his forehead.

'You say – ' he looked at Zita – 'there *was* a dead man.'

'And it was Melancholy,' Caroline said.

'Not Melancholy!' Xavier snapped at her. 'He's watching this house right now.'

'Is he?' Caroline looked away. 'You say you've heard from him, but have you *seen* him recently?'

Xavier stared at her blankly then, abruptly, rose and made for the front door. They heard him open it with unnecessary force, and then his shout. 'Melancholy! Melancholy! Come in here!'

There was a pause, then Xavier stamped back into the living-room. 'He'll come now.' He faced Caroline and Zita triumphantly. 'You'll see!'

Zita flinched involuntarily as the halting footsteps rang down the hallway and hesitated outside the living-room door. For a moment, she relived her earlier nightmare of a zombie-Melancholy summoned from his resting place by his master's command. Her eyes on the doorway, she drew a deep unsteady breath and moved to shield the sleeping Fanny with her body. Then common sense reasserted itself and she was not surprised at the figure which appeared in the doorway.

She had seen him before.

'You call?' he asked Xavier. The last time she had seen him, he had carried a triangular ladder and offered to wash her windows, while craning to see past her into the house, trying to get a good look at Fanny.

'Cheerful!' Caroline identified him, although Zita had not had much doubt who he was.

'I called Melancholy,' Xavier said. 'Where is he?'

'He's busy. I told him I'd see what you wanted.' Cheerful did not meet Xavier's eyes; he had seen the money in the open suitcase and it seemed to hold him riveted.

'I want to talk to Melancholy.' Xavier's eyes narrowed suspiciously. 'Go and tell him to come in here.'

'I told you – ' Cheerful wrenched his own eyes away from the money. 'He's busy right now.' It was as close to open defiance as perhaps any of Xavier's subordinates dared to go.

'You mean he can't come . . . right now?' Xavier asked softly. 'He's maybe . . . indisposed?'

'That's it.' A spasm that was more of a rictus than a grin twisted Cheerful's mouth.

'I see . . .' Xavier said thoughtfully. He seemed to come to a decision. 'Right!' He bent and closed the suitcase full of currency, first thriftily tucking inside the genuine bills he had retrieved from the dummy packets in the other case.

'Let's get out of here and settle this back at my place. But first – ' Xavier tore the pages of the letter and dropped them into the largest ashtray. He tossed a lighted match after them and waited for the flame to catch. It didn't, and he struck another match.

Just then, the telephone rang. The sharp peal of the bell held them all spellbound for a moment, then Zita moved to answer it. She just had time to say, 'Hello – ?' and to hear David's answering voice, when the receiver was snatched from her grasp.

'What number are you calling?' Cheerful asked. David's indignant splutter was audible across the room.

'Sorry, you got the wrong number,' Cheerful said. 'There's nobody by that name here – '

Fanny opened her eyes and looked around. She smiled sleepily at seeing Zita and Caroline – even Xavier got a drowsy acknowledgement. Then Cheerful's voice seemed to penetrate her consciousness, she turned her head, saw him – and screamed in terror.

'I don't care if you're calling from Timbuctoo,' Cheerful snarled into the mouthpiece. 'You've got the wrong number!' He slammed down the receiver and looked over at Fanny.

Fanny stared back, her screams choking off to a whimper. She clutched Romeo tightly against her and stared at Cheerful, wide-eyed. Obviously, the combination of suddenly waking from sleep and seeing Cheerful had touched a chord in her memory which had been mercifully silent earlier. Now the nightmare of what she had seen in the cottage by the river was upon her again – and she knew that it had not been a bad dream. And Cheerful knew that she realized it now.

'Yes.' Cheerful looked at Fanny, at Romeo clutched in her arms, then at Caroline and Zita. 'I thought so,' he said. 'You know, don't you?'

'We don't know anything,' Caroline said firmly. 'Whatever are you talking about, Cheerful? Wouldn't you like a drink? We're all one ahead of you.'

The telephone gave another abortive ring, choked off in mid-trill as Cheerful closed a massive fist around it and yanked the wires, box and all from the wall.

Zita felt her mind divide along two faintly hysterical tracks: What would the GPO repair man say when he saw the damage? What would David say? A man had answered her phone and hung up on him — it was the sort of thing Caroline's ex-husbands were accustomed to, but they didn't expect it in their next wives. She felt a faint glow of hope — at least, if David divorced her, it would be the end of any further association with Caroline. At the moment, it seemed almost worth it.

She drew a deep breath and came back to reality. If any of them lived through this night, they would be lucky. David was far more likely to need the services of an undertaker than a solicitor when he came to dealing with his wife — and his ex-wife.

'Fanny, don't cry, love. It will be all right.' Fanny hurled herself forward and clung to Zita, but her eyes never left Cheerful's face.

Xavier dropped the spent match he had blown out while watching Cheerful deal with the telephone and started to strike a fresh match.

'No,' Cheerful ordered, 'don't burn the letter. The

police will be very interested in it – later.' There was a gun in his hand now, pointing at Xavier. 'Leave it!'

'So,' Xavier said. 'The gloves are off, eh? The mask is dropped.' He rose to his feet slowly.

'You see – ' Caroline said triumphantly. 'I *told* you I didn't take all the money!'

'You little glutton!' Cheerful's eyes glittered savagely. 'If you hadn't tried to pull a fast one, if you'd given him the hundred thousand, it would have been all right. I'd have persuaded him that it didn't matter if you kept the other half. And, with Melancholy missing, he'd have believed me that you two were in it together and had run off. But you ruined it all!'

'You mean *you*'d have kept the other half,' Caroline said indignantly. '*I* wouldn't have had anything.'

'So,' Xavier said, his voice like the tolling of a bell. 'Melancholy is dead. You killed him.'

'He found out,' Cheerful said. 'I offered to split with him, but he wasn't having any. He was going to tell you.'

'And you knew what I'd do – ' Without moving, Xavier seemed to give off an aura of menace. Unarmed, taken unawares, he still gave the impression of being more than a match for Cheerful.

'Stay where you are!' Cheerful must have felt it, too. He stepped back involuntarily.

'We make a lot of witnesses to dispose of – all at the same time.' Xavier spoke the thought that had been in Zita's mind. Fanny clung to her with a desperate shuddering that was worse than outright sobs would have been.

'Oh, I don't know.' Cheerful did not try to pretend that he had not been considering the matter. The gloves were truly off now, the façade of civilization abandoned.

'Take an accident, now,' Cheerful said. 'More people than four can be killed when a car collides with a tree. Or goes over a cliff – by the time it reaches the bottom, who's to tell whether everyone had been conscious, or even alive, when it went over?'

'I have friends,' Xavier reminded him. 'Many friends. You would not get away with it.'

'Not so many friends as you used to have – ' For a moment, the vision of Melancholy lying beside the obsidian table shimmered before their eyes. 'And money can make friends – money and power. When I take over the clubs – step into your shoes – who is going to be rash enough to defy me? Without your backing, the others will be afraid. It will be *my* favour they seek.'

'My shoes,' Xavier said softly. 'You think you are big enough?'

'Money makes things grow.' Cheerful glanced at the waiting suitcases. 'Now I will have twice as much.'

'This is between you and me,' Xavier said. 'I do not fight women and children – nor should you. Let the others go. They will remain silent.'

'I remember – ' Fanny sobbed out suddenly. 'Zita, I can remember now. They made me drink something and I fell asleep. Then later, when it was dark out, all the shouting sort of woke me up a little – '

'Will they?' Cheerful looked across at Xavier and

shrugged. The shrug had the finality of a signed death warrant.

'It was all like part of a dream, though – ' The fatal evidence came spilling out of Fanny. 'The little fat man – the nice one – came into the room and pulled me out of bed. He wouldn't even let me get dressed, he said there wasn't time – '

'Hush, Fanny.' Zita tried to halt the revelations, but Fanny was in full flood of returning memory and would not be stopped.

'He put a blanket around me, and let me take Romeo, and carried me downstairs. He said he was taking me home. He said everything was different now and I didn't come into it any more.'

'He'd found out – ' Xavier interrupted, as though to himself. 'He hadn't had time to tell me yet, but he was clearing the decks for action, getting the child safely out of the way. He was right.'

'He was carrying me through the red, red room when the – the other one – ' Fanny indicated Cheerful – 'came up behind us and shouted some more. He said he'd share the money – that Caroline would be blamed for it all – especially if something . . . something *happened* to her later – before she could say anything to anybody – '

'Oh no!' For the first time, Caroline seemed shocked, as though full realization of the chain of events she had started were coming home to her. Perhaps she was even realizing how it might look to an outsider, how completely she had put herself into a position where anything would be – had been – believed of her.

Most of all, she seemed stunned that death had been in Cheerful's mind as far back as that – *her* death.

'The nice one said he was crazy – ' Fanny babbled on compulsively, as though she would be free of the nightmare once she had told it, not realizing that she was plunging all of them deeper into the nightmare. 'And he – ' she jerked her head at Cheerful – '*he* said something I couldn't understand – it was in another language, not English. And the nice one shouted back in that language. And then – then – he dropped me. He just sort of stumbled and dropped me – and I dropped Romeo – '

'*You* found Romeo,' Cheerful said to Zita with understated malevolence. 'What else did you find?'

'I must have hit my head when I fell,' Fanny continued. 'I can't remember anything more. Except, next time I woke up, I was some place else, and my head hurt, and I didn't have Romeo with me any more.'

'An accident,' Cheerful considered. 'They say most accidents happen in the home. Especially when there are kids around. Kids play with matches – '

'I don't!' Fanny said. 'I'm very careful.'

'No,' Zita said faintly, thinking of David's paintings, of all the paint, turpentine, linseed oil, paint rags, in the studio which would blaze so quickly and thoroughly.

'Or an explosion,' Cheerful said. 'An explosion would leave even less evidence. First an explosion, then a fire. Nobody would even get too suspicious. These are funny times and you never know who's got a little cache of gelignite tucked away for a rainy day.

Especially in a house like this – artists, anarchists, they're all cut from the same cloth.'

'And does that mean,' Xavier asked softly, 'that you have some gelignite tucked away – for a rainy day?'

Outside, the wind hurled a gust of torrential rain against the windows. Fanny whimpered and buried her face in Zita's lap. Zita stroked her head absently, wondering what their chances would be against that gun if they were all to move against Cheerful at the same time.

'I know where I could get my hands on some,' Cheerful admitted. 'If I need it . . .'

Zita spared a moment of mourning for David, who would return to find the ruins of the home he had been so proud of, to the destruction of a marriage he had been growing happy and secure in. She would not even, she realized sadly, be left her reputation. There could be no belated explanations now. David would be left to live with the worst interpretations he could put upon the interrupted phone calls, the man who answered and hung up on him. These would be buttressed by whatever fantasy the authorities might piece together about the events that had led up to the explosion and the demolished house.

It was a most unsatisfactory way to die. A way which would bequeath far more than the ordinary measure of grief and anguish to those left behind. David might never bring himself to trust anyone again. Their friends and relatives might not completely accept the idea that they had stored gelignite for some unspecified purpose – but they would always wonder.

Furthermore, it was most unfair. She and Fanny were simply innocent bystanders, caught up in Caroline's machinations. Caroline certainly had it coming – but it was a bit much to be condemned just because you were an unwitting associate of the wrong person. Zita wondered briefly if she might remain here as a spirit, haunting the site where she had previously been so happy, buttonholing those few who could see her and trying to convince them of the injustice of her untimely demise.

'Of course, gelignite might not be needed,' Cheerful said. 'There are other explosions – '

'Bullets leave traces,' Xavier said. 'The bits of us that are left might be just the bits with bullets in them.'

'That's right.' Cheerful's restless eyes had been probing the corners of the room, now they turned back to Xavier. 'That's why you're going to turn on the gas fire. But don't light it. I'll take care of that later – as I'm leaving.'

Xavier stood motionless, as though trying to out-stare Cheerful. Cheerful snapped off the safety catch on his gun.

'I'll take a chance with one bullet,' he said. 'One, they might not find. If they do, they might decide your girl-friend fired it – in self-defence – when you found the note she was trying to post to Scotland Yard and turned nasty. It's your choice. I don't mind, either way. But if you'd rather go more dignified-like, turn on that gas. Now!'

Very slowly, Xavier crossed and bent to the gas fire. During the brief seconds when his face was turned away from Cheerful and towards Caroline, Zita saw his lips move soundlessly. The only sound was the faint hiss of gas rushing through the holes in the old-fashioned appliance.

Cheerful was watching the gas fire, intent on Xavier's capitulation. He did not notice Caroline's hand creep out towards the brandy decanter again. This time, it closed around the neck of the decanter with a new purpose.

As Caroline hurled the decanter at Cheerful, Xavier leaped forward, still crouching low, to close with him as he staggered backwards, off-balance from the impact of the heavy missile.

'Yaaaay, Caroline!' Fanny sat up straight to cheer. 'Did you see that, Zita? Caroline got him!'

'Hush,' Zita said. She tried to pull Fanny down. 'Keep out of the way.'

The men were struggling for possession of the gun, the safety catch was off, a stray bullet might go anywhere. Caroline was skirting the corners of the room now, moving towards them, keeping a wary eye on the struggle raging.

'Yeah, but Caroline did it. I didn't know she could pitch like that. It was great!' Fanny was bouncing up and down in excitement.

'It was just –' Abruptly, Fanny subsided, slumping back against Zita listlessly.

'Fanny!' Alarmed, Zita looked down at the child – had some after-effect of sedation overtaken her? But Fanny was not unconscious. Her eyes met Zita's, with a pained, precocious sophistication, then turned towards the doorway.

Zita followed her gaze and found the reason she had so swiftly ceased to applaud her mother.

Somehow, in the confusion, Caroline had retrieved the suitcase full of money. Now she was tiptoeing up the stairs with it, heading towards the studio and the rooftop exit.

CHAPTER XV

LET HER GO. What did it matter? There was far worse to worry about right here in front of them. Xavier and Cheerful were still fighting. The gas was still hissing into the room at full force. Would a spark from a gunshot be enough to set off that planned explosion? It might not be as big an explosion as Cheerful had intended, but it could be enough to start a fire. The stopper had popped out of the decanter, the highly-inflammable brandy was soaking into the carpet.

'Stay here,' Zita ordered. 'Don't move.' She eased away from Fanny and off the sofa, towards the fireplace and those hissing gas jets. One thing, she determined grimly, if there *were* a fire, she was damned if she'd rescue that portrait of Caroline.

Avoiding the battle area, which had rolled over by the windows, she stooped and turned off the gas. The concentration of gas already accumulated around the fireplace made her head swim and she tried to hold her breath. If they'd just go and fight somewhere else, so that she could open the window –

The shot had a dull, curiously muffled sound. Xavier and Cheerful were so interlocked it was impossible to tell which had fired the gun, which received the bullet.

Zita returned to Fanny and they watched in dread as one began to shake himself free of the other.

On second thought, Zita reached out and firmly annexed the heavy brandy decanter herself. Anything Caroline could do . . . Fanny gave her a wan smile.

The winner rose groggily to his feet and looked around. He seemed to notice the gun still in his hand and grimaced with distaste. He pulled a handkerchief from his pocket and carefully polished the weapon free of fingerprints before laying it down on the arm of a chair.

From the chair, his eyes travelled to the floor, to the spot where the case containing his money had stood. He did not appear particularly surprised to find it empty. He transferred an abstracted look to Zita and Fanny.

'Where is she?' Xavier demanded.

Zita shrugged mutely. Fanny set her mouth in a stubborn line, conveying that no torture could drag the information from her. However, her eyes instinctively rolled ceilingwards, giving the game away.

'I see,' Xavier said. 'What's upstairs?'

There was no use shrugging in answer to that question, she could not claim ignorance of the layout of her own home.

'The bedrooms,' Zita said reluctantly, 'the bathroom, my husband's studio.'

'Another way out?'

'The studio opens on to the roof. There's a fire escape to the ground at the end of the terrace. She – she could go along the rooftops and – '

Xavier was no longer there. He had whirled and dashed up the stairs. Zita was staring after him when

Fanny whimpered suddenly.

She turned in the direction of Fanny's gaze to see Cheerful lurch to his feet, blood oozing from a wound in his side. He looked past them, staring at the doorway through which Xavier had vanished. Eyes fixed on the doorway, he moved forward with a grim determination not even the pain or loss of blood could weaken.

Zita shrank back, pulling Fanny down, as he stumbled past them, but he did not seem to notice they were there. Here, she realized, was the zombie-like figure which had been haunting her imagination. Despite his uncertain steps, he moved almost soundlessly, the drops of blood from his wound leaving a dark red trail across the carpet.

She would have to have a new carpet, she decided, trying to keep hysteria at bay. Even if blood and brandy could be removed without trace, she could never bear to look at that carpet again

Fanny clung to her, obviously fighting her own hysteria. To move or speak might be to divert that monomaniacal murderous attention towards themselves. At least Xavier had a head start – and it was possible that the stairs might defeat Cheerful in his desperate condition. Silently, fearing to break the spell, they watched his progress.

He halted only once. At the chair, to pick up the gun. Then he was in the hall. They heard him stumble and fall against the stair rail then, painfully, begin to pull himself up the stairs.

Should she have done something? And what could

she have done? Zita became aware of the overpowering smell of gas, the muzziness in her head. Almost as slowly as Cheerful, she rose and crossed the room to open the windows.

'Fanny,' she called. 'Come and get some air.' She leaned out the window herself, breathing deeply. In a moment, Fanny joined her. There were noises overhead, carried down to them like the rain on the chill night air. They seemed distant, far away, and nothing to do with her. She continued to fill her lungs with the fresh damp air, feeling her head clear gradually as oxygen replaced the gas in her system. They must have inhaled more of the noxious stuff than they had realized. In a minute, when she was feeling stronger, she must leave the house, find a telephone, call the police. And she must take Fanny with her – the danger of pneumonia was less now than the danger that it might be Cheerful who returned from that rooftop rendezvous, still anxious to get rid of any witnesses.

A scream shrilled down from above. Not a scream of terror, but one of mortal anguish – from which, Zita deduced that someone was trying to part Caroline from the money again.

'Caroline!' Still retaining enough remnants of innocence to keep her from accurately pinpointing the nature of her mother's scream, Fanny stiffened. 'They're hurting Caroline!'

Before Zita could realize her intention, Fanny backed away from the window and darted like quicksilver for the stairs.

'Fanny – come back!' Zita dashed after her.

Fanny flew up the stairs. By the time Zita had reached the studio, Fanny was already on the roof. Mercifully, she stood frozen there, just outside the studio door, staring aghast at the combatants who were perilously close to the edge of the slippery wet roof.

Quietly, Zita stepped up behind and got a firm grip on Fanny's shoulders. Then she, too, caught her breath as she watched the scene before them.

Caroline and Xavier were silhouetted in intermittent blue flashes against the rain-sodden sky. They appeared to be having a tug-of-war over the suitcase. Neither of them seemed aware that Cheerful was lurching towards them, trying to steady the gun in his hand in order to take aim.

But at which one?

Zita's grip on Fanny tightened as she seemed to be about to start forward. But Fanny responded to the silent warning, stepping back, clasping her hands over her own mouth lest she cry out and startle Caroline.

Cheerful stumbled again as he moved forward. The gun spun from his hand and lost itself in the blackness of the night. There was an indeterminate thud as it landed – somewhere on the roof.

Cheerful regained his footing, peered around vaguely for his gun, then seemed to abandon the effort. Revenge must have been uppermost in his mind. He raised his head, focusing with difficulty on the oblivious figures swaying on the edge of the roof.

Then, with an inarticulate bellow of rage and pain, he lunged forward.

They all teetered wildly for a moment on the edge

of the roof, against a blue-lit sky, then – as though in slow motion – gradually tipped over the edge and disappeared.

There was one final scream from Caroline – this time a scream of genuine fear. Then silence.

'Downstairs!' Zita said. This time, she was in the lead as she and Fanny plunged through the studio, down the stairs to the ground floor and out into the street.

Pulling the front door open, the thought occurred to her that the curious blue lightning was still flashing all around them, with no accompanying thunder. But she lacked the ability to follow the thought through right at that moment.

Cautiously, trying to hold Fanny back, she advanced on to the pavement. Cheerful was crumpled in the middle of the street, as though the force of his rush had carried him outwards and beyond the others.

Caroline was stretched out gracefully across a crumpled shape that must be Xavier. Even the awkward twist of her head above a grotesquely curved neck did not dispel the illusion of fragile beauty.

The suitcase must have broken open as they pitched off the roof. Five and ten-pound notes were still fluttering down slowly towards the ground. Some caught and nestled in tree branches like new exotic birds, some swirled around the roots of bushes making the most expensive compost heaps in the world, others drifted earthwards in a leisurely manner – a summer snowstorm of negotiable currency, wasted on its observers.

Zita became aware that there *were* other observers. That the blue lightning was flashing from the lamp atop a police car, that the police themselves were staring at the scene with something like awe.

'Cripes!' A young constable surfaced beside her, giving an opinion which would not appear in his written report to his superiors.

'Here – ' his partner rushed up to them – 'we'll have to order a couple of ambulances for this little lot. There's another dead 'un in the car parked across the way. Rigor's set in already.' He shook his head and pulled out his walkie-talkie.

'Melancholy,' Zita murmured, but they paid no attention. Or perhaps they thought it her own comment on the situation – a bit flowery, but not unsuitable.

As they watched, the still unconscious Caroline stretched out her hand in a convulsive reflex action and clenched it around a packet of ten-pound notes.

'This is the first time,' the young constable said, in the tone of one conscious of making police history, 'we ever had a 9-9-9 call direct-dialled from New York City.'

CHAPTER XVI

VISITING HOURS were so unrestricted as to be non-existent. After two weeks on the critical list, Caroline was now improved enough to be allowed general visitors. Naturally, they were all going to see her. It would be a pity if poor dear Caroline were to feel neglected, wouldn't it? What a shame if friends and admirers weren't to rally round and tell her how wonderful she looked, how marvellous she was, how glad they were that she had come safely through –

'Oooww!' Fanny said. 'You're pulling my hair.'

'Sorry, love.' Zita disentangled the comb and tugged more gently at a stubborn snarl. 'But you want to look nice for your mother, don't you?'

'Mmm.' Fanny wriggled uncomfortably. 'I suppose so, but – '

'But what?'

'Oh, I don't know.' Fanny thought for a minute. 'I mean, *you* seem more like a mother than Caroline does. A *real* mother. Caroline is more like a sister.' She thought again and amended. 'A *little* sister.'

'Do you know – ' Zita looked at Fanny in some surprise – 'I believe you're right.' Fanny was growing up – something Caroline would never do. Caroline would grow old without ever growing up. It would, in the long run, be harder on those around her than on Caroline.

'Zita – ' Fanny had been thinking again. 'I'm half-English, aren't I?'

'That's right.'

'Then, when I'm grown up, I can come back here and live?'

'That's right.' It was faintly amazing that Fanny should be thinking of that, after all she had been through here.

'Good.' Fanny exhaled a sigh of relief. 'I'd like that. England is a *fun* place.'

So much for childish traumas. Fanny was made of sterner stuff than the case histories in psychology studies. Also, Zita reflected, Fanny had been luxuriating lately in being an only child. Her behaviour had improved, she had found friends of her own age in the neighbourhood, she was learning to hold her tongue, she had even shown signs of trying to be helpful. By the time she returned to California at the end of the summer, she would be unrecognizable. It was, quite possibly, a triumph of environment over heredity.

'Ready?' David appeared in the doorway, seeming as anxious to get under way as though he hadn't been a daily visitor for the past week. It was a bit much, really, for Caroline to have listed him as her next-of-kin.

'Coming.' She gave Fanny a little push. 'Get your cardigan.'

'And Alfa,' Fanny said. 'Caroline hasn't seen Alfa yet. It will be a surprise for her.'

'She might have a surprise for you,' David said indulgently. He and Fanny had attained an entente

cordiale since his return which seemed to surprise
them both. 'Just you wait and see.'

They let Fanny run ahead to have a few minutes alone
with her mother. Also, Zita had several questions she
wanted answered before she faced Caroline again.

'Isn't this –' she looked around suspiciously – 'an
awfully *expensive* nursing home?'

'Mmmm.' At times, David could be as evasive as
Caroline.

'Do the police usually put up their prisoners in such
expensive places?'

'She's here as a private patient,' David said. 'It won't
cost the ratepayers a penny. And anyway, she isn't a
prisoner. More of a material witness, if anything.'

'What do you mean material witness? Aren't they
going to charge her?'

'Well, they've been having a bit of trouble trying to
decide what crime she's actually committed. Xavier
refused to press charges on the theft. He may be
deported anyway – if he lives. And Cheerful committed
the murder, but he'd have died from the gunshot
wound, even if he hadn't gone off the roof. Caroline
didn't have anything to do with that – you testified
to that yourself.'

'So I did,' Zita said grimly, remembering the endless
question and answer sessions, while Caroline lay unconscious and untroubled in hospital – leaving someone
else to hold the baby, as usual.

'And then the police have been aching to get rid of
Xavier for a long time. They aren't going to be too

harsh on anyone responsible for finally getting him out of their hair. And those lawyers of Caroline's helped, too – you noticed how the publicity was soft-pedalled?'

'I noticed.' It was the one thing to be grateful for in the whole situation. 'But it isn't fair. Caroline was to blame for the whole thing. None of it would have happened if she hadn't taken that money.'

'Oh, I don't know. Cheerful must have had the idea of taking over from Xavier at the back of his mind for a long time. Caroline just accelerated matters – and she *did* have a close call. The police and doctors weren't at all sure she'd pull through for a while. I think she looked so frail and helpless she brought all their protective instincts to the fore . . . you know Caroline.'

'I know Caroline,' she agreed. 'They'll probably wind up giving her a medal. Just tell me one thing: this expensive nursing home, those lawyers you mentioned – who's paying for all this?'

'You'll meet him in a minute.' David grinned wryly. 'Like the song says, "*They've got an awful lot of coffee in Brazil.*" '

'They'll need to have,' Zita said.

'This is Jaime,' Fanny greeted them as they came through the door. 'It's not a surprise – it's just another father.' She brightened slightly. 'But he says I can have a horse of my own when I come to visit them.'

'Jaime, darling – ' Caroline waved her right hand towards David and Zita – her left hand was pinned to the coverlet by a Brazilian emerald as big as a paper-weight on the third finger – 'these are my dear, dear friends.'

It was easy to see why Caroline had defected in favour of the more glamorous Xavier. And yet, as Jaime came towards them, a controlled strength in the gnarled face, a certain shrewdness in the dark twinkling eyes suggested that there might be a deeper reason. This was not a man who would allow a woman to use him as Caroline had used Xavier. His indulgence was measured, it would be withdrawn if his standards were not met. Caroline was going to have to mend her ways, or else risk losing more than she was accustomed to wager in her little games.

'Practically her family, I am told.' Jaime's face creased in a smile that made Zita wonder uncomfortably if he had read her thoughts. 'You must come and visit us in Brazil.'

'Yes, do,' Caroline agreed. 'You'll love it, David – you've never seen such things as there are to paint there. We'll take you on a trip into the Interior – the jungle foliage, the animals, the wild orchids, the fantastic plumage on the birds, the – '

Zita stole a sidelong glance at David. He seemed to have gone into a trance, listening to the sirens singing. He was lost in the dream world Caroline had created, as though he were already squeezing out the vivid colours on to the palette, hearing the screams of the macaws above the roar of the Amazon. It was irresistible to an artist.

'Say you'll come, Zita,' Fanny pleaded. 'You can go

horseback riding with me.'

'You see – ' Jaime shrugged. 'We all wish it – and we are a family who get what we want.'

'We'll give you a lovely portrait of Caroline for your wedding present,' Zita decided firmly. 'And David can paint a Brazilian scene for the mantelpiece.'

'Actually,' David grinned, recognizing the bargain and accepting it, 'I've been thinking of doing a portrait of you to put in that spot.'

'Then it's settled!' Caroline exclaimed. 'Oh, I'm so happy!' She beamed at them all fondly.

'When is the wedding?' Zita asked, with a trace of anxiety.

'As soon as possible,' Jaime said. 'And then I will take my poor little broken bird and fly home with her, where she will recover her health and her strength.'

Zita fought down an unworthy feeling that Caroline didn't deserve to be happy. Caroline had a charmed life – that was all there was to it. Other people could die from falling down a few steps. Not Caroline – not even falling from a roof had finished her. She had come out literally on top. On top of Xavier, who had broken her fall and saved her life.

Caroline was not totally unscathed. One leg was in traction, and her neck had been broken. Even now, her delicate face emerged from an enormous orthopaedic collar like an overframed cameo.

'Dear Jaime – ' Caroline stretched out a hand – 'you're going to spoil me most dreadfully.'

He came to her side, taking her hand and beaming down at her. 'I will try to.'

'She'll make very sure that he does,' David whispered into Zita's ear, squeezing her hand.

'And dear, *dear* Zita – ' Caroline stretched out her other hand – 'what would I have done without you?'

Across the bed, Zita met Fanny's oddly-adult amused gaze before she looked down into the guileless wide violet eyes looking up at her trustingly. *Little sister –* Fanny was right. Caroline was the child, and always would be. She would rush headlong at life, through other alarms, other excursions, growing old without really growing up. And yet, life would have lost some of its colour and been duller if she had not survived.

Brazil was not that far away, as flying time went. Caroline, Fanny – and now, Jaime – were inextricably interwoven into the fabric of their lives.

'*Dear* Caroline – ' Did the others hear the trace of irony in her voice as she took Caroline's hand? Recognizing a graceful defeat, yet not resenting it, Zita resignedly faced it, and what it entailed.

A future through which they would all walk – as they were now. Hand in hand . . . in hand.

If you have enjoyed this book and would like to receive details of other Walker mystery titles, please write to:

Mystery Editor
WALKER AND COMPANY
720 FIFTH AVENUE
NEW YORK, NY 10019